5069001 W9-APM-733

Gulley, Philip

A lesson in Hope : a novel

This book has been donated in

memory of

Elaine Berry

by The Family of
Elaine Berry

A Lesson in Hope

ALSO BY PHILIP GULLEY

A Place Called Hope

A Lesson in Hope

A Novel

PHILIP GULLEY

**CENTER
STREET**

New York Boston Nashville

Center Street
Hachette Book Group
1290 Avenue of the Americas
New York, NY 10104

CenterStreet.com

Printed in the United States of America

RRD-C

First Edition: September 2015

10 9 8 7 6 5 4 3 2 1

Center Street is a division of Hachette Book Group, Inc.
The Center Street name and logo are trademarks of Hachette Book Group, Inc.

The Hachette Speakers Bureau provides a wide range of authors for speaking events. To find out more, go to www.HachetteSpeakersBureau.com or call (866) 376-6591.

The publisher is not responsible for websites (or their content) that are not owned by the publisher.

Library of Congress Cataloging-in-Publication Data has been applied for.
ISBN: 978-1-4555-1984-2

To Joan

Acknowledgments

With thanks to the good people of Center Street, Steve Hanselman, and Stacey Denny.

A Lesson in Hope

1

$\smile$

S am Gardner had been the pastor of Hope Friends Meeting a scant four months when Olive Charles, aged ninety-eight, drew her last ragged breath and, in the general consensus of Hope Friends, went to be with Jesus. Sam had no opinion on her destiny, having met her on only four occasions at the nursing home where she resided. She hadn't said a word and had appeared dead then, truth be told. So when the funeral home had phoned Sam at 6 a.m. on a Monday, his day off, to report her demise, he hadn't been at all surprised.

Her funeral was held at the meetinghouse that Saturday. She had never married, but did have one niece in Chicago whom she hadn't seen in twenty years, who showed up at the funeral bawling her eyes out at the sight of Olive lying stiff in her casket. She recovered quickly, pulled Sam aside, and asked him if the will had been read. She reeked of alcohol and her speech was slurred.

"I have no idea," he told her.

"Do you know if Aunt Olive had any other relatives? I've

kind of lost touch with the family. Did anyone ever come visit her at the nursing home?"

"Just me and folks from the meeting," Sam said.

"Did she say anything about money?"

"Not to me, but then she'd stopped talking about a year ago."

"We were very close," the niece said. Sam hadn't caught her name—Ramona, Regina, Rowena, he wasn't sure—and after only five minutes with her had no interest in learning it.

Ruby Hopper, the clerk of Hope Friends Meeting and its resident saint, phoned Sam later that same afternoon to ask if she could bring the message the next morning.

"You certainly may, if you feel led."

"Thank you. Olive and I went on vacation together for many years. I'd like to show slides from our trips."

"Oh, I see."

"Do you think that would be all right?"

"It sounds like a wonderful tribute to a well-deserving member," Sam said, more than happy to have Ruby man the pulpit since it meant he wouldn't have to write a new sermon for the next Sunday.

There was a sizable crowd at meeting the next morning—the usual modest crowd plus a half dozen guests, a few of them on the verge of membership who hadn't yet been tricked into joining. They sang several songs, and Sam prayed, then turned the pulpit over to Ruby.

"I wanted to take this opportunity to share about Olive Charles, whom we lost this past week. Olive was one of our founding members. Very kind. Very dedicated to the meeting. We vacationed together until three years ago, when her health turned. She was an absolute joy."

"Smart, too," Hank Withers added, when Ruby paused to breathe. "She was on the Building Committee when they hired me to design the meetinghouse. She would have made an excellent architect."

Hank was a retired architect and thought it high praise indeed that Olive could have been similarly employed.

They watched slides, projected on the wall behind the pulpit. Ruby and Olive at Niagara Falls, Mount Rushmore, the Lincoln Memorial, and the Alamo. Halfway through, Ruby began to weep, so Sam finished the narration while Ruby sobbed beside him. She eventually recovered, and Sam prayed, thanking God for Olive, then Ruby hurried to the kitchen and began serving pie, a custom Sam had come to appreciate. The morning ended on a high note, with everyone admitting Olive had lived long enough, that it had been her time to go, and that it had probably been a blessing. Homemade pie could cast a positive light upon the most tragic event.

Sam took Monday off, and was in the office early Tuesday morning when the phone rang. It was Olive's attorney, serving as the executor of her estate, phoning to inform Sam that Olive had left her beloved Quaker meeting her entire estate, consisting of one house and its contents, a 1979 Ford Granada with four snow tires, barely used, and a bank account a dab north of eight hundred thousand dollars. Sam had never cared for lawyers, but in that moment felt a general warmth toward the profession and probably would have hugged the man, had they been in the same room.

Ramona, or Regina, or whatever her name was, phoned a few minutes later, screeching about suing the church and everyone in it and coming down there and getting what was rightfully hers, since she'd been the only one who'd ever loved

Olive. Sam let her rant a little while, excused himself, and hung up the phone.

Sam Gardner loved nothing more than to be in possession of a juicy morsel of news no one else knew, so he savored the situation for several minutes, sitting in the quiet of his office, then phoned the members of the church, summoning them to an emergency meeting that evening. He couldn't tell them over the phone. He had to tell them in person, all at once, so they would hear the same thing. He would see them at seven.

"Should I bring a pie?" Ruby Hopper asked.

"Several," Sam said. "Can you make one of those apple pies with the crumbly things on top?"

"A Dutch apple pie? I certainly can."

It was shaping up to be the finest day Sam Gardner had ever had in all his years of ministry.

His wife, Barbara, was at work, at Hope Elementary, where she served as the librarian. Sam walked the five blocks there, caught her in between classes, and told her what had happened.

"That's two hundred thousand dollars a visit," he pointed out. "Not bad for an hour's work."

"Sure beats library pay," Barbara said.

"Her niece is madder than a wet hen. She called to tell me she's going to sue the meeting and everyone in it."

"This is the niece who hadn't seen her in twenty years?" Barbara asked.

"That's the one."

"They come out of the woodwork when they sniff a little money, don't they?"

Sam was too distracted to work, and spent the rest of the day fending off curious church members who'd happened to be in the neighborhood and so dropped in to visit.

Wilson Roberts waddled into Sam's office and plopped down on the couch. "Is the yearly meeting going to throw us out?" he asked. "They better not, that's all I can say. Not five years ago, I donated a brand-new toilet and sink for the superintendent's office. They throw us out and I'm going over there and taking them back."

"No, the yearly meeting isn't throwing us out," Sam said.

"Then why did you call a meeting?"

"You'll find out tonight, along with everyone else. I don't want to have to tell the story a dozen different times. You'll have to be patient, Wilson."

When Wilson realized he couldn't wear Sam down, he took his leave. No sooner had he gone than Wanda and Leonard Fink stopped by. Sam's phone call had wakened them, they had been speculating ever since, and had concluded Sam had become an atheist and was announcing his resignation, which didn't trouble them in the least. Indeed they were relieved, and not at all surprised, because they had seen a book on his office shelves entitled *The Pastor's Secret: The Rise of Doubt among Clergy.*

"We know what the meeting is about," Wanda Fink said, cutting to the chase.

They probably do, the big snoops, Sam thought.

"I would prefer not to discuss it right now," Sam said. "I only want to tell it once."

"I never thought I would live to see the day when something like this would happen," Leonard said. "Have you given any thought to what this will do to our church?"

"I've been thinking of nothing else," Sam said. "It will be a test for us, that's for sure. But I prefer not to say anything more until tonight, when everyone is present."

"How can you sit there and be so calm?" Wanda said. "It's like you don't even care."

"I care a great deal. I just don't think it's anything to get all worked up about. It's happened to other churches and they dealt with it. So will we."

"We? What do you mean *we*? You're not planning on staying, are you?"

"I most certainly am," Sam said. "The meeting needs steady leadership at a time like this."

Wanda and Leonard stormed from the office. As long as he lived, Sam would never be able to figure out some people.

2

I wonder if I'll get a raise," Sam said to Barbara over supper. "Remember when I interviewed? They said they'd love to be able to pay me a higher salary, but that they didn't have the money."

"That would be nice," Barbara said. "College isn't getting any cheaper."

"I sure am glad you got your librarian job at the school. I don't think we could make it without that."

Levi, their older son, was at Purdue University, where he had switched his major four times in three semesters. Engineering, then sociology, then back to engineering, and he was now, to his parents' dismay, studying theater. Yet another college major that assured a future of want.

Addison, their youngest, was in the Army, had made it through basic training in Oklahoma, and was stationed in Texas, where he was learning to kill people with a chop to the throat.

"I hope they don't put the money in a bank and never do anything with it," Barbara said. "It could do so much good."

About the Contributors

Shelley Ann Rice-Wyckoff, Chair of the Social Work Department, Alabama A&M University

Rebecca Turner, Vice President for Academic and Student Affairs, Jacksonville University, Alabama

Phyllis Ivory Vroom, Dean of the School of Social Work, Wayne State University, Michigan

Earlie M. Washington, Dean of the College of Health and Human Services, Western Michigan University

Joyce Z. White, Director of the School of Social Work, Marywood University, Pennsylvania

"I hope they don't fight over it," Sam said. "The Finks stopped by the office and they're already worked up about it."

"How did the Finks know? I didn't think you were telling anyone until tonight."

"Oh, you know them, they're nosy. They probably sniffed it out."

"I wonder how someone manages to save up eight hundred thousand dollars," Barbara said. "I can't imagine having that much money."

"According to Ruby, Olive lived simply, never married, and never had children. She only had the one brother, but he died young, before her parents, so she probably inherited all the family money."

"I wonder why she didn't leave anything to her niece."

"Because she has a drug and alcohol problem," Sam said.

"Oh my, that's terrible."

"At least that's what the lawyer told me. He said, and I quote, 'Apparently, Olive had a niece, but declined to leave her any money because of her history with drugs and alcohol.'"

"That is so sad. I would be sick if our children ever did that. Maybe the church should give her Olive's house."

"So she can sell it and buy more drugs and booze and kill herself," Sam said. "Not a good idea."

"What in the world is the meeting going to do with Olive's house?"

"Sell it, I imagine," said Sam.

"That means we'll end up with close to a million dollars," Barbara said.

They discussed various possibilities for the money, getting themselves worked up at the thought of it. Sam was imagining an office suite with an administrative assistant and an associate pastor to do the visitations so he wouldn't have to. Barbara had in mind more virtuous endeavors, such as feeding the hungry and helping children born with extra arms or cleft palates or things such as that.

"Well, if you don't mind, I think I'll stay home from tonight's meeting. I don't want to see a bunch of Quakers bicker over money," Barbara said. "But take good notes. I want to know what everyone said."

"Will do."

Though the meeting wasn't until seven, everyone was there by six thirty, chomping at the bit.

"What do you have to tell us, Sam?" asked Hank Withers, not giving Sam even a moment to shed his coat.

"He doesn't believe in God, that's what he's going to tell us," Wanda Fink said.

"And he still wants to be our pastor," Leonard Fink added.

While it was true Sam had occasional misgivings about God, he had been feeling rather positive about their relationship, especially since that morning.

"Let's meet in the kitchen, where the pie is," Sam suggested.

They clustered around a folding table, including Dan and Libby Woodrum, who hadn't yet joined the meeting, but were under intense pressure to do so, which was why Sam had invited them. Even Ellen Hadley, the clerk of the church's pie committee, was present. She hadn't attended worship services for three years, but still felt free to make her opinions known.

"I heard from Olive Charles's attorney this morning—" Sam began.

"Oh, Lord, we're getting sued," Leonard Fink said. "That's it. We might as well close our doors. This is terrible, just terrible."

"We're not getting sued," Sam said.

"Do they expect us to pay her nursing home bills?" Wayne Newby asked. "We can't do that."

"Wayne, put a cork in it," Ellen Hadley said. "Go on, Sam."

Sam was starting to appreciate Ellen Hadley.

"As I said, I received a phone call this morning from Olive's attorney. He is serving as the executor of Olive's estate. Apparently Olive has left eight hundred thousand dollars to us, plus her house and furnishings, and her 1979 Ford Granada."

They stared at one another in stunned silence.

Wayne Newby was the first to speak. "I'll take the Ford Granada."

"Why should you get it?" Leonard Fink asked. "Did you ever think someone else might need a car?"

"Let's not bicker," Ruby Hopper said. "We need to give this a great deal of thought. Could we please enter into silence and center ourselves?"

It was a noble thought, which everyone but Ruby ignored.

Hank Withers said, "Friends will no doubt remember that when we built our meetinghouse the original design called for a slate roof, which we couldn't afford at the time. Our roof is the original roof, and desperately needs to be replaced."

"As the clerk of the roof committee, I would support that suggestion," Wayne Newby said. "And as long as we're on the topic, I'm willing to pay the meeting four hundred dollars for the Granada."

"It's worth every bit of two thousand," Leonard Fink said. "You trying to cheat your own church?"

"Now that I think about it, we shouldn't have to pay for a new roof," Wayne Newby said, smoothly changing the subject. "I think we have hail damage. We can get insurance to buy us a new one."

"I was up on the roof just last month. There's no hail damage," Hank Withers said.

"There can be," Wayne Newby said. "All I need is a broomstick and a couple of hours."

"We're not going to cheat our insurance company," Ruby Hopper said.

"They expect it," Wayne said. "It's figured into the cost of insurance. It's not cheating if they expect it."

"We ought to give serious thought to a fellowship hall," Hank Withers said. "Our original plan called for it. We could do a lot more things if we had a fellowship hall."

"We need a new stove in the kitchen. A gas one this time," Ellen Hadley said. "Those electric stoves are worthless. And it should be commercial grade, like they have in restaurants."

"The women's restroom needs a new countertop," Wanda Fink said. "Someone used the wrong type of cleaner on it and it's all scratched up."

"Just the other day on the Internet I saw a Ford Granada going for a thousand dollars. I guess I could pay that much for it," Wayne Newby offered.

"Let's all settle down," Sam said. "We don't even have the money yet. The executor said it might take up to six months, maybe a year, to settle the estate. And that's if no one sues. Her niece phoned this morning and threatened to do just that."

That threw a bucket of cold water on the matter.

"Well, whenever it gets settled, I have dibs on the Granada," Wayne said.

Leonard Fink frowned. "Why should you get the car? Maybe I wanted to buy it. Did you ever think of that?"

"No one has dibs on anything," Ruby Hopper said. "We must establish a process and follow it. As the clerk of the meeting, I recommend we appoint a committee to decide the best use of this unexpected gift. Do Friends approve?"

"Approved," they rumbled.

"Who feels called to serve on that committee?" Ruby asked.

Fifteen hands went up around the table.

"You're not a member yet, Sam," Wanda Fink pointed out. "Only members can serve on a committee."

"I've applied for membership," Sam pointed out. "We're just waiting on a letter of transfer from Harmony Meeting."

"The Woodrums aren't members, either," Leonard Fink observed.

Dan and Libby studied the floor, embarrassed.

"We're sorry, we just wanted to help," Libby said.

They bickered about membership for a while, half of them arguing it shouldn't be a requirement for service, the other half fighting to the death to preserve a tradition they hadn't given a moment's thought before.

"I've been a member of this meeting since it first started," Wanda Fink said. "My parents were members of their meeting, and their parents before them. Now you're telling me membership doesn't matter. I don't even know if I can go here any longer."

The rest of them sat quietly, contemplating the happy prospect of Wanda Fink's departure.

The meeting broke up at nine o'clock, with Wanda threatening to bolt, and the committee membership still undecided.

If Olive Charles had still been alive, Sam would have wrung her scrawny little neck for donating so much money to the meeting, and said so to Ruby Hopper after everyone had left.

Ruby chuckled. "Don't you worry, Sam. They'll settle down. But next time someone leaves the meeting almost a million dollars, let me know first, so we can present this in the right way. You just can't dump something like this on everyone all at once."

"I'm sorry. You're right. I should have told you first."

"Well, it's nothing we can't work through. I'm sure everything will turn out all right."

Which, for a woman of Ruby's intelligence, was a terribly naïve sentiment. And, as it turned out, a great miscalculation.

3

～

Sam arrived early at the meetinghouse the next morning. He'd spent the previous day preoccupied about the money, so was now behind in his work. He was compiling a list of recent visitors, following up with handwritten letters inviting them to return. An hour or so into the task, he heard a steady thumping on the roof.

Probably falling walnuts, he thought.

The noise continued, and Sam remembered they didn't have any walnut trees. He pulled on his coat and walked outside, peering up at the roof, where he saw Wayne Newby punching the shingles with the end of a broom handle.

"What are you doing?" Sam called up to Wayne.

"None of your business," Wayne yelled back.

"That can't be good on our roof."

"Yeah, who knows, we might get a new roof out of the deal," Wayne said. "Looks a lot like hail damage."

"Wayne Newby, you stop that right now," Sam said. "That's out-and-out fraud."

"This is none of your business, Sam. I'm the clerk of the

roof committee. Now leave me alone to do my job. And you better not tell anyone, either, or you'll be finding yourself a new clerk of the roof committee. Just pretend you didn't see this."

"For Pete's sake, we're a church. We can't cheat our insurance company."

"We've been paying insurance on this building since 1984 and never once filed a claim," Wayne said. "They jack the rates up every year. It's about time we got a little something in return."

Sam paced back and forth in the yard. "We could go to jail for this."

Wayne harrumphed. "I should have done this at night when you weren't around. I knew you wouldn't have the stomach for it."

Sam returned to his office, and the knocking resumed for several more minutes, followed by a louder thump and a scream. Sam hurried outside, where he saw Wayne Newby sprawled on the ground, his right leg bent at an unnatural angle. Wayne was pasty white, working his mouth like a landed fish but making no sound.

Sam bent down over him, checked to see if he was breathing, then ran inside to phone 911. A fire truck and ambulance arrived within minutes. Wayne had found his voice and was screaming in pain. The paramedics transferred him to a flat board, loaded him in their ambulance, and hauled him away. The firefighters stayed behind to finish the paperwork.

"What happened?" a firefighter asked Sam.

"He fell off the roof," Sam said.

"He looked too old to be climbing around on a roof. What was he doing up there?"

"He's the head of our roof committee. I think he was in-specting the roof for damage."

It was an outright lie, which made Sam a coconspirator. He had a fleeting image of sharing a prison cell with Wayne Newby for the next twenty years.

Sam excused himself and phoned Doreen Newby to tell her that her husband had been injured while committing a crime. He called Ruby Hopper, who was properly appalled, then drove to the hospital to meet Doreen there. Sam arrived first, and found Wayne in the emergency room. He had been given an IV, and was filled with painkillers and in a positively cheerful mood.

Sam was less than happy. "If anyone asks what you were do-ing up on the meetinghouse roof, I'm going to tell them the truth. Just look at the mess you're in."

"It was worth it to get these drugs," Wayne said. "I feel wonderful."

"Yeah, well, when they wear off, you won't feel so good. Maybe then you'll come to your senses."

Wayne grinned at Sam, pleasantly out of his mind. "You're a good pastor, Sam. We're lucky to have you."

Doreen Newby bustled into the room, saw Wayne, and flipped him in the ear, hard, the Quaker-wife equivalent of a smack upside the head.

"Wayne Newby, I told you not to get up on that roof at your age. Now look at you. You're lucky it's only a broken leg. You could be dead."

"We can't be seen together," Wayne said. "My wife might find out."

"What are you talking about?" Doreen demanded.

"He's delirious from the painkillers," Sam explained.

"If my wife finds out about us, we'll both be goners," Wayne said.

Sam excused himself from their marital spat and went to sit in the waiting room. It was the same hospital where his sons had been born, so after a while he wandered upstairs to the maternity ward and searched for their names. The hospital had charged Sam ten dollars to etch each son's name and date of birth on a plastic plaque, which was then affixed to the wall. Thousands of names, dating back to the 1940s, lined the halls. It took him ten minutes to find their plaques, and he stood before each one for several moments, remembering the days they were born. If today he discovered Barbara was pregnant, it wouldn't bother him in the least. Except that he'd had a vasectomy ten years before. That might bother him a bit. But he would get over it once the baby arrived. Children were fine additions to any home, and he missed his every day.

Addison phoned most every Monday evening to chat. Sam and Barbara waited by the phone, and would pick it up on the first ring and put it on the speaker so they both could listen. Addison would report on his day, then ask about theirs, then speculate about where he might be stationed. He was hoping Alaska, so he could see a glacier before they all melted.

As for Levi, he had informed them the night before that he was changing his major, for the fifth time, to construction management, which seemed to Sam to be a good fit. As a child Levi had spent countless hours playing with Legos and Lincoln Logs. At the age of five, he had sawed the legs off their kitchen table. Yes, construction management seemed a fitting career for their older son.

After daydreaming about his sons, Sam made his way back to the emergency room to check on Wayne and see if he and

Doreen were still married. Wayne was asleep, and Doreen was filling out insurance papers.

"I've half a mind to walk out and never speak to him again," she told Sam. "I think he's having an affair."

Sam had known Wayne Newby only four months, but he doubted there existed a woman who might see him as the doorway to Nirvana. Unless she was attracted to overweight men in their late sixties who wore engineer caps and played with model trains in their basements.

"People say unusual things when they're under the influence of drugs. I'm sure he's been faithful to you."

"You think so?"

"I'd bet my life on it," Sam assured her.

He sat with Doreen into the early afternoon, then excused himself and returned to the meetinghouse, where he occupied himself until four o'clock, when Barbara arrived home from work. They exchanged news about their days, each trying to top the other. Sam won easily, Wayne's falling off the roof during the commission of a felony easily trumping a kindergartener who'd wet his pants.

"He was knocking holes in the shingles to mimic hail damage?" she asked, incredulous.

"Yep."

"Well, it serves him right," Barbara said.

"That's kind of what I thought, too."

Then their phone rang, and Sam answered it.

"Pastor Gardner, this is Jack Shear, the attorney for Olive Charles's estate. Do you have a moment to talk?"

"Sure. What's up?"

"It's about Olive's will. It's been challenged by her niece. She's hired an attorney. We might have a problem on our hands."

4

〜

A surgeon operated on Wayne the next morning, pinning his broken leg. Sam drove to the hospital to sit with Doreen and found most of the congregation with her in the waiting room, playing euchre while they waited to hear from the doctor.

"So what was Wayne doing on the roof?" Hank Withers asked Sam. "I understand you saw the whole thing happen."

"He was hitting the shingles with the end of a broomstick, trying to make it look like hail damage," Sam said. "I guess he lost his balance and fell."

"How far did he get? Do you think we can get a free roof out of it?" Hank asked. "When you think about all the money insurance companies make, it doesn't seem all that wrong to get a new roof from them. They'll never miss that money. It's pocket change to them. I'm filing a claim."

"Good idea," Wilson Roberts said. "They'll never miss that money."

A nurse approached to tell them Wayne was being wheeled into surgery, which sent a slight ripple of excitement through the group, with various of them predicting all manner of problems Wayne might encounter during the operation. Wanda Fink told about an aunt who had died on the operating table during a routine hernia repair, then Wilson Roberts recalled how a neighbor had caught a bacteria while in the hospital that caused his flesh to be eaten by unseen but vicious microbes. Hank Withers topped them all with a story he'd read in a magazine at the grocery store checkout counter about a surgeon's going berserk and killing *his patient and the nurses and everyone in the waiting room!* It had happened somewhere in China or India or Pakistan, Hank couldn't remember for sure, but he knew it was true.

Sam suggested they have a moment of prayer for Wayne, even though he wasn't sure God was all that enthusiastic about the outcome, given the circumstances surrounding Wayne's injury. It would be the same as praying a bank robber made a clean getaway. Sam thought it would certainly be a test of God's grace if Wayne survived the operation. He didn't say this out loud. Instead he asked God to forgive Wayne for trying to cheat the insurance company, that he'd done it with the best of intentions, to help the Church, the Bride of Christ, and since he'd been trying to help God's daughter-in-law, then maybe God could forgive Wayne and help him through the surgery. Amen.

"Well, I don't know what good that prayer will do," Doreen Newby said. "If God didn't know what Wayne was up to on that roof, he sure does now, thanks to you ratting him out."

"That's an interesting observation," Hank Withers said. "Did God not know Wayne was a cheat until Sam told him? I thought God knew everything there was to know."

They bickered for a while about whether God knew everything, even before it happened, and if God did know someone was getting ready to do something bad that would send them to hell, then why didn't God do the kind thing and strike them dead before they did it?

Sam excused himself after a few minutes, signaling for Ruby Hopper to follow him into the hallway, where he told her about Olive's niece's hiring a lawyer to challenge the will.

"Did Olive's lawyer seem concerned?"

"He simply said we might have a problem on our hands," Sam told her. "That's all I know so far."

"Will he keep us informed of the situation?"

"I'm sure he will," Sam said.

"Then let's just wait and see what happens. I'm sure this isn't the first time a will has been challenged."

"Changing the subject," Sam said, "what are we going to do about Wayne?"

"What about Wayne?"

"We have the clerk of the roof committee attempting to defraud an insurance company, and Hank and Wilson are all for it. We can't allow that. I'm not a prude, and I've bent the truth a time or two myself, but we can't intentionally commit fraud. It's not right."

"I'll talk with Wayne when he gets out of the hospital," Ruby said. "But he can be stubborn."

"What about Hank and Wilson?"

"I'll speak to them, too," Ruby promised.

They returned to the waiting room. The doctor emerged to tell them the surgery had been a success and that Wayne would spend several days at the hospital, then be released to a rehabilitation center for physical therapy.

"I guess God thought Wayne's heart was in the right place

after all," said Hank Withers. "Looks like Wayne is going to be okay."

Everyone hugged Doreen good-bye and promised to bring her food, then left the hospital together, heading toward their cars.

"What's on your plate the rest of the day?" Hank asked Sam.

"I have a pastors' luncheon to attend. All the Quaker ministers in the area meet four times a year for lunch. Today's the day."

"Well, enjoy yourself then. We'll see you Sunday, if not before," Hank said.

Whether Sam enjoyed himself at the pastors' luncheon depended entirely upon which pastors attended. He liked all of them, except two, who made him want to renounce the Christian faith and take up Buddhism. One was his superintendent, who had been a decent guy until he'd become the superintendent, then had gotten mad with power. The other was an older minister, Otis Pringle, who'd crippled every church he'd ever pastored, and now drifted from church to church, full of himself, leaving bloodied, broken spirits in his wake, as if spirituality were a contact sport. Otis had not yet joined any church Sam had pastored, though he had threatened to attend. In the event he did, Sam had concocted a plan to deal with him. Invite Otis to return to the meeting-house the next morning for a visit, conk him on the noodle, hard, roll his big butt up in a blanket, put him in the trunk of the superintendent's car, then place an anonymous call to the police a day later, accusing the superintendent of murder. Two birds with one stone.

He had discussed the plan with Barbara, who had thought

for a moment, then said, "Make sure you wear a stocking hat and gloves, don't leave any DNA behind, and burn the clothes you do it in."

To his relief Otis Pringle was absent, but the superintendent was present, and gracious to the point of smarminess, which made Sam suspicious. He apologized to Sam for being less than helpful in his transition to a new congregation and wished him every blessing at Hope Meeting. He admitted they had gotten off to a bad start, but hoped they could enjoy a congenial partnership in the years ahead. Sam reached back to see if his wallet was still in his back pocket.

"I understand the Lord has blessed your meeting with a generous financial gift," the superintendent said.

"That would indeed be a blessing," Sam said, neither confirming nor denying the statement.

"We hope to renovate the yearly meeting headquarters, and will be inviting some of our more prominent congregations, like yours, for instance, to consider a generous gift."

"I'll be sure to let the elders know," Sam said, because laughing and saying, "Fat chance of that happening" seemed a bit rude.

"The Lord bless you," the superintendent said, extending his hand in a beatific gesture as if someone had declared him pope.

Sam took a seat between two of his pastor friends. Good people, steady, faithful, not too creative, but compassionate. The kind of pastors you would want to have show up at the hospital if you'd just been told you had a flesh-eating bacteria and were being eaten alive by unseen but vicious microbes. They reported their Quaker meetings were doing well, not growing, but not dying, either. Hanging in there.

"Heard you got a wad of money," one of them said to Sam.

"Where did you hear that?" Sam asked, impressed by the efficiency of the pastors' gossip network.

"A member of my meeting has a sister in your congregation. I think her name is Wanda. Anyway, Wanda told her sister and her sister told me."

"I see."

That probably explained how the superintendent knew.

"Wanda told her sister your meeting was going to send the money to missionaries."

"No decision has been made yet," Sam said. "In fact, I'm not counting on anything until we get the money, which isn't going to be anytime soon."

"If my meeting had that kind of money, I'd run off with it," Sam's friend said. "And if I didn't do that, I'd at least try to get an assistant so I wouldn't have to prepare bulletins anymore. I hate bulletins."

Every minister Sam knew despised preparing the weekly bulletin. He wondered why churches that did the exact same thing week after week even bothered with bulletins. The only things that changed were the songs, which were announced anyway. *Let us now stand and sing hymn number seventy-eight.* As if they weren't going to stand unless there was a footnote in the bulletin that read, "Those who are able, please stand." It wasn't the only question Sam had about why churches did what they did, though it was near the top.

After the pastors ate, each one stood and described a positive development at their Quaker meeting, which took considerable thought for some of them, but they rallied nicely and talked about an especially nice funeral or potluck dinner. Sam mentioned the uptick in attendance at the monthly pie suppers, then rather cryptically said he might have good news in six months or so, but until then wasn't at liberty to say anything. He glanced at the superintendent, who was hanging on Sam's every word, leaning forward like a ravenous wolf eyeing a tender lamb.

5

Olive's lawyer phoned late the next morning.

"Jack Shear here," he said to Sam. "It's just as I feared. Olive's niece, Regina Charles, has retained an attorney. I received a registered letter from them informing me of their intention to sue unless she gets half the money and sole possession of the house."

"Have you spoken with them?"

"Not yet. I wanted to speak with you first, and give you the opportunity to talk with your church."

Sam sighed. Nothing was ever easy.

"Do you know this Regina Charles?" Jack Shear asked.

"I met her briefly at Olive's funeral."

"What was your impression of her?"

Sam thought for a moment, recalling their meeting. "Well, when she first saw Olive in the casket, she cried like her best friend had died. Then she pulled me aside, asked if Olive's will had been read, then wanted to know if Olive had any other relatives, and whether or not Olive had ever mentioned having any money. Plus, she smelled like a brewery."

"I see this all the time. Someone dies and relatives come out of the woodwork."

"What do you recommend we do next?" asked Sam.

"As I said, talk with your church and see what they want to do. My duty is to defend the will and see that Olive's wishes are carried out. However, it might be in your best interests to offer her niece a relatively modest sum of money, perhaps fifty thousand dollars, and hope she goes away. Most of the time, that does the trick. The lawyer pockets a third of it, which in this case would be around sixteen thousand seven hundred. That's not bad pay for writing one letter."

"Okay," Sam said. "I'll check with the church and get back to you. But they'll probably want to know whether Olive's niece has any chance of winning a lawsuit."

"It all depends," Jack Shear said. "The law on this is very clear, and judges are inclined to honor wills. But if the niece claims the church manipulated Olive to get her money, it could get messy. Judges don't like it when older people are taken advantage of."

"We had no idea she even had any money, and wouldn't have treated her any differently had we known."

"Doesn't matter. Olive's not here to say otherwise, so it's your word against her niece's word. A judge might be inclined to split the estate down the middle as a matter of fairness. That's why it might be wise to offer her a settlement and hope she goes away."

Sam hated what money did to people, hated that it turned otherwise kind people into grubs. He was starting to wish Olive had left her money to cats or the Girl Scouts or a secret love child, the product of a romantic tryst with a shoe salesman when she was thirty-five and visiting Des Moines.

Having learned his lesson, he phoned Ruby Hopper first, shared the news, then e-mailed the rest of the congregation to announce another emergency meeting that evening. Two emergency meetings in one week. He hoped this wasn't indicative of his future—squabbling over money.

This time he set the meeting for four o'clock, hoping people would conclude their business quickly and hurry home to supper. Everyone arrived on time, Sam explained the situation, then suggested they offer Regina Charles fifty thousand dollars, per their attorney's advice.

"That would buy us a slate roof," Hank Withers pointed out. "I don't think we ought to give her one thin dime. In all the years Olive was in the nursing home, her niece never visited her. Not once."

"I saw something like this in a movie once, where this relative showed up out of nowhere trying to get some money, and they hired someone to kill him," Wilson Roberts said. "They made it look like a car wreck. Got away with it, too."

"I have a brother who's a beekeeper. Maybe we can get some of his bees to swarm her. They sting her, she goes into shock, and she's gone, just like that," Leonard Fink said, with a snap of his fingers. "Happens all the time in Mexico. That'll teach her not to mess with the Lord's money."

"We're not going to kill anyone," Ruby Hopper said. "I can see why Olive's niece is upset. It never feels good to be left out. And we don't know the reason she never visited Olive. Perhaps there was a family fight we knew nothing about. I think we should err on the side of grace and offer her half of Olive's estate. That way we can use our share of Olive's estate in good conscience."

"I can spend all of Olive's money with a perfectly clear conscience," Hank Withers said. "Let's not forget our dream of having a fellowship hall. This would pay for it."

Ruby Hopper, as it turned out, was a party of one, the rest of them feeling perfectly free to cut Regina Charles off at the knees. Sam, still harboring the fantastical illusion that he might get a raise before all was said and done, was starting to regret he'd suggested giving Regina fifty thousand dollars.

"I say we hire a lawyer to protect our interests," Wilson Roberts suggested.

"Waste of money," Sam said. "It's the executor's job, in this case Olive's attorney's job, to make sure the will is carried out as written. So our interests are already protected because of his legal duty."

The others were clearly impressed by Sam's legal expertise, and he modestly said, "Pastors must be educated about a number of things."

They snarled back and forth another half hour, the tide turning against Regina, whom they had come to despise without even knowing her. Ruby Hopper was the sole saint, and so was quickly getting on their nerves. If a vote had been taken, they might well have let Leonard's beekeeping brother include her in the swarm.

Over Ruby Hopper's objections, they decided to stick it to Regina Charles and not give her a dime. By then even Sam despised her and was perfectly content to throw her to the wolves.

"It isn't right," Ruby said. "We didn't even know this money existed a few days ago, now it's made us selfish and uncaring. We're better than this."

They sat quietly, considering her words, apparently decided they could live with themselves, and held firm.

6

A memory.

When Sam turned ten, his grandpa had hired him to mow his lawn.

"Don't tell your father I'm paying you," he'd warned Sam. "He'll make you give the money back. Every boy needs a little walking-around money."

It took Sam an hour to push-mow the yard, then a half hour to trim around the trees and flowerbeds, all for the princely sum of five dollars, which was serious money in those days. But the best part came afterward, eating lunch with his grandparents, then sitting on their front porch swing, scrunched between them, surveying the lawn with its neat rows, drawing in the pleasant odor of cut grass.

One Saturday his grandpa was unusually quiet. Spoke hardly a word during lunch, then excused himself from the porch-sitting to go sit in the garage.

"What's wrong with Grandpa?"

"We got a phone call this morning that his brother, Ernie, died yesterday," Sam's grandma explained.

"I didn't know Grandpa had a brother Ernie. What relation would he be to me?"

"Well, Ernie was your daddy's uncle, so that made him your great-uncle."

"How come I never knew about him?" Sam asked.

"That's probably a question you should ask your grandpa."

So Sam, being ten and curious, not understanding the importance of tact and sensitivity, walked out to the garage and asked his grandpa how come he'd never told him he had a brother.

"There are some things that are private," his grandpa had said. "And that's one of them."

"Why is it private? Why can't you tell me?"

Sam had an insatiable curiosity and continued to badger his grandfather, hoping to wear him down.

"Didn't you know you had a brother? Did your parents keep him hidden from you? Is that why I never heard about him?"

His grandfather sighed. "You never knew about Ernie because I never told you about him. I didn't tell you about him because my brother and I haven't seen one another in over thirty years. We had a fight and stopped speaking."

"Roger and I fight all the time, but we still talk to one another," Sam pointed out.

"It's different when adults fight. Kids have a fight and forget all about it in five minutes. Adults remember."

"What did you and Ernie fight about?"

"An inheritance."

"What's an inheritance?"

"It's something people leave their friends and family when they die. Money and furniture and land. Things like that.

Things they won't need anymore since they're dead," his grandfather explained.

"Did you and Ernie fight over furniture?"

"That and other things. Mostly money. We were in our forties and Mom and Dad died, one right after the other. Mom, that would be your great-grandma, got breast cancer and died. Dad, your great-grandpa, died six months later. Just gave up, I guess."

"And that's when you and Ernie had your fight?"

"Not right then. But a year or so later, he wanted to buy the family farm. We bickered about the price, it got nasty, and the next thing you know it was Thanksgiving and we didn't get together as a family and we just stopped talking to one another. Stupid, stupid, stupid. And now he's dead, and we can't talk."

He looked at Sam. "Make me a promise."

"What?"

"Promise me you'll never fight over money. It isn't worth it."

"I promise."

It had been an easy promise for Sam to make, since he'd had no money, and few prospects of acquiring any in the near future.

He and his grandfather had never discussed Ernie again, but every now and then since that day Sam had wondered about the other Gardners. Wondered how they looked, where they lived, what they were like. A time or two he'd asked his father, who'd had only a few vague memories of long-ago family reunions. They had exchanged Christmas cards with a cousin for a number of years after the split, but even that had stopped.

"From what I understand, none of Ernie's kids wanted to farm, so they sold it out of the family, Ernie and his wife moved down South, and I have no idea where my cousins are.

Wouldn't know them if they kicked me in the shins," Sam's father had told him.

It is hard to miss what you've never had, so Sam seldom thought of his cousins, except at Thanksgiving, when it was just he and his folks and Barbara and the boys and Sam's brother Roger and Roger's girlfriend, if he had one at the moment. To be accurate, he didn't think of his cousins specifically, what he thought about was the vacuum, the void, what should have been but wasn't. He thought of his promise to his grandfather on days like that, never to fight over money, and wondered whether arguing over money was ever worth it. He didn't know for sure, but was leaning toward not.

The night of the church meeting, lying in bed, Sam said his prayers and added an extra one, asking God to make him kind. And wise, he added. Kind and wise.

7

The Gardners' phone rang early the next morning. Sam and Barbara were lying in bed, waiting until the last minute to get up and going.

"Are you going to get that?" Sam asked.

"You know it'll be for you. Why don't you just get it?"

"Maybe it's Publishers Clearing House and we've won ten million dollars."

"That never happens."

Sam reached it on the fifth ring. It was Doreen Newby, calling to report Wayne had an infection, was mad with fever, and they'd had to sedate him. His toes had turned black and Doreen was afraid they would have to lop off his foot or even his leg or maybe just take everything off below the waist.

"Are you at the hospital now?" Sam asked.

"Yes, I'm here. Room 2126."

"I'll be right there," Sam said.

He showered, dressed, ate a quick breakfast, hurried to the hospital and up the stairs to Wayne's room, where he found Wayne unconscious. Doreen sat beside him, holding his hand, anxious, afraid, and eager to talk, which she did for the next three hours, describing her various illnesses. After a bit Sam fell asleep, though Doreen didn't seem to notice. He had drifted off during Doreen's recitation of childhood measles and awakened to learn of her mononucleosis at the age of fifteen. He had slept for an hour and she had covered only six years. It promised to be a long day.

"They call mononucleosis the kissing disease, but I never kissed a boy until I met Wayne. We were nineteen, working as camp counselors at Quaker Haven. He was a real dreamboat. All the girls wanted to date him."

Something had obviously happened to Wayne, Sam thought. Something bad. Sam couldn't imagine women dreaming about him. His gut hung over his belt, hair sprouted from his ears, and his eyebrows were grown together. Fifty-some-odd years ago, maybe he had been a looker, but those days were gone.

Sam and Doreen went downstairs to the hospital cafeteria for lunch. When they returned, Wayne's doctor was in the room, studying his chart, looking faintly pleased.

"All the blood tests came back. I think he's going to be all right. He needs to lose weight, and get serious about his diet. Did you know he has diabetes? Before he leaves the hospital, he'll have to meet with a dietitian and learn how to control it. I'll also have medicine for him to take, but I'll explain all that when he's awake. In the future, he would be well advised to stay off roofs. He's lucky he didn't hurt himself any worse than he did. With his diabetes, he won't recover as quickly, so we're going to keep him here another couple days."

Doreen began to weep. Sam patted her on the back, then said a prayer over Wayne, asking God to heal him and keep him from doing anything stupid, like climbing around on roofs.

He bid Doreen good-bye, promised to stop by the next day, then headed back to his office. In all the excitement of the possible inheritance, Sam had not yet seen Olive's house, so phoned her attorney for the address, which he supplied, along with the observation that it was a lovely home, in excellent repair, and likely to fetch three hundred thousand dollars, perhaps more, on the open market.

Olive's house was less than a mile from the meetinghouse, on a curvy, treelined street with the houses set well back from the road. The house had a broad front porch and a detached garage off to the side, with oak and maple trees scattered on the lawn. Two stories, with lots of carpenter's lace, and built, from what Sam could judge, sometime in the late eighteen hundreds. Sam pulled over to the curb.

There was a van in the driveway, the rear door was standing open, and Regina Charles, Olive's niece, came through carrying a table lamp. Sam watched as she carried it to the van, then went back inside, emerging a moment later carrying a small table, which she also deposited in the van. She was a hefty woman, outweighing Sam by a good fifty pounds. He didn't think it wise to challenge her, so phoned Olive's attorney instead.

"I'm at Olive's house and her niece appears to be emptying the place," Sam told him.

"Have you asked her not to?"

"I'm not going anywhere near her," Sam said.

"I'm calling the police right now to report a burglary in progress. I'll be there in ten minutes with a copy of the will."

He was as good as his word, rolling up to the curb just

as the first police officer arrived. In that short time, Regina had hauled a toaster, a television, and a computer to the van, and was wrestling a dining room table through the front door, while the attorney introduced himself to the police officer, produced the will, and explained that Regina was looting the place. Sam stayed well behind the officer, trying to decide whether to video the proceedings with his phone just in case someone was killed.

When Sam was living in Harmony, it had been the general consensus that crime was an everyday event in the city, that scarcely a day passed without everyone's witnessing a murder or mutilation of some sort. It had taken four months, but it appeared Sam would finally see something gory. He had seen murders before, but only on television, in Westerns, and the dead guys always recovered and were back on television the next week.

The officer approached Regina, asked to see her identification, called in her name for outstanding warrants, then asked her to stay put on the porch while he searched the van. By then another officer had arrived and Regina was screeching about her rights. She made a run for one of the officers, swinging her purse, hitting him upside the head, knocking him into a rose-bush. She walloped him once again for good measure, then turned on the other officer, who hadn't eaten as many dough-nuts, was a bit more nimble, and managed to jump out of the way, pull his stun gun, and run fifty thousand volts through Regina, causing her to flop on the sidewalk like a headless chicken.

Sam was hiding behind his car, so he didn't see any of it un-til that night when it appeared on the evening news. Jack Shear, Olive's lawyer, had recorded it and sent it to a television station. Sam had hoped to take credit for subduing Regina, which became impossible when the broadcast showed him hiding behind his car, his hands over his eyes, yelling for his mother.

"I'm a lover, not a fighter," he told Barbara, after she'd snotted herself laughing at him.

"It's probably a good thing you didn't challenge her," Barbara conceded. "She appears to be psychotic."

"She's not doing herself any favors."

"I think it's sad. She probably doesn't have a dime to her name. Maybe the church should give her something."

"She'd just waste it," Sam said.

"Oh, and the church won't? You watch and see. They'll piddle it away."

"Your lack of faith in the church troubles me." Sam had grave doubts about the church, too, but from time to time enjoyed acting pious at someone else's expense.

Though it had been a dramatic day, he fell asleep immediately and dreamed he'd been given a raise, and that for the first time in his pastoral career he was finally being paid a living wage. It was, however, only a dream.

8

Wayne Newby was sitting up in bed the next day, bright-eyed and eager to leave the hospital.

"Has the insurance company been by to see the roof?" he asked Sam.

"No, they have not, and they're not coming by. We're not going to cheat our insurance company. How's your leg?"

"Hurts. And itches, too. I can't scratch it with this cast on."

"I didn't think they used casts anymore," Sam said. "I thought they just shot people with broken legs, like they do horses."

Wayne's chin began to quiver. "I was all set to go to a model train convention in Louisville this weekend, but the doctor told me I can't go. Been waiting for it all year, now this had to happen."

Sam thought of quoting the Bible about the wages of sin' being death, or at least a broken leg, but it was apparent Wayne felt bad enough, so he kept quiet.

"I'm just glad it wasn't worse," Sam said. "You could have landed on your head or broken your neck."

"Yeah, I guess I was lucky. I never should have gotten up on that roof in the first place."

Wayne finally seemed sorry for trying to cheat their insurance company. Sam took him by the hand. "Fortunately, God forgives us."

"Well, I should hope so. I was trying to do the Lord a favor, after all."

So much for repentance and getting right with the Lord. Sam made a mental note to preach on the subject of repentance more often. He had never been big on that topic at Harmony Friends, given Dale Hinshaw's tendency to expound on it at every opportunity. But from what Sam could tell, the nearer one lived to a city the more likely one was to sin, so a rousing sermon on repentance might be fitting. A dab of hellfire, a scorch of flame, to keep folks on the straight and narrow.

After leaving the hospital, he stopped by Jack Shear's law office to check on the status of the meeting's inheritance. No news there. Regina's lawsuit hadn't been tossed out.

"She'll get her day in court," Jack Shear said. "Unless we can settle it out of court."

"Is she still in jail?"

"So far as I know. If she hadn't attacked the officer, they probably wouldn't have arrested her," he said. "But once you slug an officer with your purse, that pretty well guarantees you a night or two in the slammer. She's lucky they didn't shoot her."

"I've been thinking more about it," Sam said. "And even though I think she'll waste it, I'm going to try to talk the meeting into giving her part of Olive's estate."

"Again, as the executor of the estate, it's my job to see that Olive's wishes are carried out. But I think everyone's best interests can be served if we're able to reach an agreement out of court. There's no telling what a judge or jury will do if the case gets that far. So go ahead and see if you can't encourage the meeting to make her an offer. Otherwise this money could be tied up for years. Not that I mind, since I get paid by the hour."

"Who pays you?"

"The estate. Three hundred dollars an hour."

Sam couldn't imagine making that much money an hour. He had once kept track of his hours to figure out his hourly pay and had come in at a dollar above minimum wage. Three hundred dollars an hour was unthinkable. He should have become a lawyer. More money and weekends off.

By the time Sam made it back to his office at the meetinghouse, it was well past lunch. An unfamiliar car was sitting in the parking lot. A Mercedes. *Probably an Episcopalian*, Sam thought. He had mastered the art of determining someone's religious faith by the car they drove. No Quaker he knew drove a Mercedes. They might want to, but it wouldn't be worth it for all the grief they would get.

"I wonder how many children might have been fed for what that car costs?" their fellow Quakers would muse aloud.

Or "It appears the Lord has blessed you, though you wouldn't know it from what you've been giving to the church."

Or "I had a cousin who bought a car like that. He went bankrupt a few years later and the bank came and got it."

Definitely an Episcopalian car, or a well-heeled Methodist. Perhaps a Congregationalist. Or a member of the Mafia.

The door of the Mercedes swung open and a man emerged. He was wearing a shiny black suit, pointy shoes, a blue shirt with a white collar, and a gold ring big enough to gag a camel. His hair was heavily gelled and slicked back. *Mafia*, Sam thought.

"Are you Sam Gardner?" the man asked.

"Yes. Why do you ask?"

"I'm Todd Cameron. I'm representing Regina Charles."

A lawyer. Even worse.

Sam studied him, not saying anything.

"I've come to talk with you about my client. While attend-ing her aunt's funeral at your meetinghouse, my client fell on your uneven sidewalk and injured her back. She's been unable to work ever since and has retained me to seek justice on her behalf."

"What uneven sidewalk?"

"Right over here," Todd Cameron said, pointing out where the sidewalk had heaved up a quarter of an inch. "When a sur-face appears to be level, our feet barely lift when we walk. Even the slightest protuberance can cause us to trip."

"I would imagine the risk is heightened if the person walk-ing is drunk or high the day she tripped. If she did trip, which I didn't notice, and I watched her leave."

"She'll be seeking one million dollars in damages, plus her legal fees, of course. Her injuries have left her unable to work. She's in constant pain, and unable to find relief."

"A million dollars. That's a convenient figure."

"I think you'll discover it's a reasonable figure once you learn the extent of my client's injuries."

He handed Sam his business card, took several pictures of the sidewalk, then wished Sam a pleasant day, which wasn't likely to happen.

"By the way," he said, turning toward Sam as if it were an afterthought, "since you're the pastor, you're also being named in the suit."

9

What do you mean we're being sued? Who would sue us? We haven't done anything."

"Regina Charles is suing us, along with the church, for one million dollars," Sam explained to Barbara, as she walked in the door.

"What in the world for?"

"She claims she tripped on the meetinghouse sidewalk, hurt her back, and is unable to work. So she found a lawyer and is coming after us. Some guy named Todd Cameron."

"You're kidding. I've seen his commercials on television. He's a shark."

"That's the one," Sam said.

"Well, you can't get blood from a turnip. I guess this is one time it's nice not to have anything."

"I hope he doesn't get wind of my pocketknife collection," Sam said, his face clouded with concern. "I'd hate to lose that."

Sam phoned Ruby Hopper, who wasn't home, so he left a message on her answering machine, telling her they were in big

trouble, that the church was being sued for a million dollars it
didn't have, and that they'd probably have to close their doors.

"I probably ought to fix that sidewalk so no one else trips,"
he told Barbara.

"That's not your job," Barbara pointed out. "Call Hank
Withers. He was the architect in charge of the building project.
Tell him to fix it."

Hank arrived within an hour, mixed cement in a wheel-
barrow, then troweled it out onto the walk, bringing it level.
Sam stood and watched him, amazed, unaccustomed to this
efficiency from a church trustee. Every other church he had
ever pastored had had lengthy procedures for such things. It
would have been passed from one committee to another for a
year or so, with each person weighing in, offering an opinion,
citing a relevant verse of Scripture, suggesting various relatives who were in the cement business and might give them a
discount.

"That ought to do it," Hank said, smoothing the last bit of cement. "But I'll tell you right now, that was not large enough to
trip over. Well within code. She's just looking for a quick buck."

"What a mess," Sam said. "I don't have money to hire a
lawyer."

"Don't worry about it. Our church policy covers you in
an event such as this. That's what Olive's niece and her attorney are counting on. They know you don't have deep pockets.
They're going after the insurance money, the big cheats."

"Oh, I see. Kind of like what Wayne was doing," Sam observed. "Trying to cheat the insurance company."

"It's not exactly the same thing."

"It sounded the same. Defrauding insurance with a bogus
claim."

"Somehow it seems all right when it's an insurance company," Hank said.

Sam laughed. "Yeah, it does feel like poetic justice, doesn't it?"

"Sure does," Hank said. "But maybe we shouldn't cheat them anyway."

"Probably shouldn't," Sam agreed.

"You ministers sure know how to put a damper on things."

"That's our job. To squelch joy and ruin the best-laid plans," Sam said.

They talked for a while about Regina Charles, agreeing it was going to be a big mess, then cursed lawyers to the depths of hell, and expressed delight in the nobility of their chosen vocations, architecture and ministry.

They stretched a rope around the fresh cement so no one would step in it, then sat in Sam's office, speculating about Olive Charles's house and what it might be worth. Hank was of the opinion it would easily fetch three hundred thousand dollars on account of its location.

"We wouldn't want to rent it, would we?" Sam asked.

"Do you want to be a landlord? I don't. It's all I can do to keep my own place going," Hank said.

"Maybe we could put Wayne in charge of it," Sam suggested. "It would serve him right."

"Nah, let's not. Then every month at our business meeting we'd have to listen to a report about it. Every time we had to repair or replace something, we'd have to have a long discussion about it. It would be a nightmare."

"Didn't think of that," Sam admitted. "I hate meetings. Let's unload it as quick as we can."

"That's what I'm thinking."

They sat in a pleasurable silence for a few moments, looking out at the beech trees.

"There's something you need to know," Hank said, his voice lowering. "But for now I'll ask you to keep it to yourself."

"What's going on?"

"Norma's been diagnosed with Alzheimer's."

"Oh, Hank, I'm so sorry. When did you find out?"

"Last month. This past year, I noticed she'd been having trouble recalling certain words. Then she stopped socializing and doing her daily activities. Kept forgetting where she put things. Couldn't remember names anymore. The neurologist is pretty sure it's Alzheimer's. Her mother had it, too."

"Have you told anyone else?"

"Yes, we told Ruby Hopper. She suspected it already. She and Norma are pretty close. But we haven't told anyone else in the meeting. Norma doesn't want everyone fawning all over her."

Sam had never understood the reticence often associated with illness. When he was suffering from a malady or misfortune, he wanted everyone to know it. If, in the usual course of conversation, someone didn't ask him how he was doing, he told them anyway. He admired people who faced their suffering stoically, but he wasn't one of them.

"Does she know that I know?" Sam asked.

"Yes, she said I could tell you. But as I said, she doesn't want it to get any further."

"I understand. No one will hear it from me. Can I mention it to Barbara?"

"Sure, you can tell Barbara. But tell her not to tell anyone else."

Sam told her that evening over dinner, after she complained about having a headache.

"It could be worse, you could have Alzheimer's like Norma Withers," Sam said.

"Norma has Alzheimer's? When did you find that out?"

"Today. Hank told me. He told me not to tell anyone but you, so keep it to yourself."

"When was she diagnosed?"

"Last month. Apparently she started having these bad headaches."

"Headaches?"

"Yeah, she'd get them in the evening. Right around this time of day, interestingly enough. That's when they first realized something was wrong."

Barbara frowned. "You're a twerp. Alzheimer's is nothing to joke about."

"You can either laugh or cry," Sam said. "Might as well laugh."

They discussed Alzheimer's and other dreadful diseases and what they would do if they got them.

"Suicide," Sam said. "If I found out today I had Alzheimer's, I'd stick my head in our oven."

"Our oven is electric," Barbara said. "All that would happen is that you would singe your hair. Or what's left of it."

"Well, I'd do something. I'm not sticking around if I get Alzheimer's, I'll tell you that right now. I'm checking out."

"If you want, I can help you," Barbara said, but she smiled when she said it.

"Might take you up on that. Maybe we can make love so vigorously I'll die of a heart attack. Now that would be the way to go."

"Don't count on that happening," Barbara said. "If I had a terminal illness, I would be so noble about it that after I was dead everyone would talk about how brave I was and someone would donate a million dollars in honor of me and they'd name a building after me. Maybe a library or a school."

"Don't count on that happening," Sam said.

All in all, it was a pleasant evening, talk of death making them profoundly grateful to be alive.

10

For the second time that week, Sam was awakened by a phone call from Doreen Newby, who announced she needed to talk with Sam, pronto, and would be at his office in a half hour. She was curled in a knot of grief on his office couch when he arrived, clutching a letter to her chest, sobbing. She thrust the letter at Sam. "Read this, and tell me why I shouldn't leave him."

June 4, 1981

To Wayne, the love of my life,

I look forward to the day we can be together for good. I know it will be hard to tell your wife about us, but I will make it up to you.

We're young yet, and have the rest of our lives together. I promise to give you the love you've always wanted, but have never been able to find until we met.

Yours forever,
Vicky

"Where did you find this?" Sam asked.

"Underneath the lining in Wayne's sock drawer. With him in the hospital, I decided to clean and organize his dresser. And I found this."

"I'm so sorry, Doreen. This must hurt a great deal."

Wayne Newby was bald and lumpy, had hair sprouting like weeds from his ears, and, as it turned out, was a no-good cheating bum from way back. Nevertheless, Sam felt it important, if only for Doreen's sake, to put the matter in perspective.

"Doreen, this letter is over thirty years old. And Wayne obviously didn't leave you. And this is a letter to him, not from him. Who knows, this woman Vicky might have been stalking him. Perhaps it was all one-sided."

"Then why would he have kept the letter? It meant something to him, otherwise he would have thrown it away."

She had him there.

Sam was in no mood to defend Wayne Newby, but neither did he want to see Doreen and Wayne divorce, divorce being a ton of work for pastors—having to visit both parties, listen to their venom about each other, phone each of them daily to see how they were doing. Sam hated divorces.

"Have you asked him about it? There might be a perfectly reasonable explanation."

"I'm in no mood to talk to him. I'm not even sure I want to see him again," Doreen said. "I've never been so humiliated in all my life. I was foolish not to see it."

"What was there to see?" Sam asked. "Had he been acting oddly?"

"He's always acted oddly. He's in his seventies and still plays with toy trains. He's nuttier than a fruitcake."

"I mean, did he act like he was having an affair? Did he hang up the phone when you came into the room? Was he gone a lot without explanation? Have you noticed money missing or unusual charges on your credit card? Any suspicious e-mails? Lipstick on his shirt collar, that sort of thing?"

"No, nothing like that," Doreen admitted.

"Then he's probably not having an affair."

"There was a Vicky who used to attend here. She moved about twenty years ago. She was always flirting with him. I wonder if it was her?"

"Vicky is a pretty common name. I'm sure you have nothing to worry about," Sam assured her. "Why don't you just ask Wayne about it so you can stop worrying?"

"Can you go with me to talk to him?"

Ugh. If there was anything Sam hated more than divorce, it was involving himself in a marital spat. Things got ugly quick.

"Why don't you talk with him first, then if you would like, perhaps after Thanksgiving, I'll meet with both of you," Sam suggested.

Sam had noticed that marriages tended to blow up around Thanksgiving and Christmas, when husbands and wives spent a lot of time together and got annoyed with one another.

"Forgive my poor memory, but how many children do you and Wayne have?"

"Two, a son and a daughter. And four grandchildren. And if they knew the truth about their father and grandfather, they'd be devastated."

"What are your plans for Thanksgiving?"

"They were coming to our house for the Thanksgiving weekend, but I think I'll call it off."

"I was thinking just the opposite. You need to be sur-rounded by people who love you, and that includes your husband. I do think he loves you. This is an old letter, he didn't leave you, which is a positive sign. People have moments of weakness. But if something happened with this Vicky woman, and I'm not saying it did, it happened over thirty years ago. She's obviously not a part of his life now."

It took Sam a good hour to calm Doreen, by which time he was wrung out. It had been a busy few days—a hospitalized parishioner, a case of Alzheimer's, and a possible divorce. He was comforted somewhat by the proverb that trouble came in threes, though he would learn soon enough that proverbs weren't always true.

11

That evening, just as he was relaxing, his mother phoned to tell him she and his father were coming to their house for Thanksgiving, and had invited his brother and his current girlfriend to come along.

"Tell Barbara we'll bring all the side dishes and pies," his mother said. "We're anxious to see your house. I can't believe we haven't seen it yet. It's been four months. I guess you've been too busy to invite us."

"You know how it is, Mom. Moving in and everything. Getting Levi back to school. Starting a new job. But we'll be glad to have you."

"We thought we'd spend the weekend with you, and come to church on Sunday. We miss hearing you preach."

"Who's preaching at Harmony now?"

Sam had pastored Harmony Friends Meeting for fourteen years, and though he had left under difficult circumstances, he still carried a torch for his hometown meeting.

"Oh, the superintendent sent some dried-up old nub of a man who's got one foot in the grave. It's all I can do to go."

"What's his name?"

"Some potato chip name. Lays or Ruffles or something like that."

"Do you mean Otis Pringle?" Sam asked.

"Yes, that's his name. Otis Pringle."

"Otis Pringle has killed every church he ever pastored. I don't understand why they let him anywhere near a pulpit."

"Well, he's carrying on that tradition here. We're down to about twenty people on Sunday morning."

It pained Sam to hear that. All that work, fourteen years spent building up a congregation, to have it undone in scarcely a year's time.

"You all need to get a new pastor, and quickly," Sam told his mother.

"The superintendent said he wants Otis to be here for four years, then retire. Then he wants his nephew to come here."

Sam groaned. "He's a bigger idiot than Otis Pringle. He's the worst kind of idiot. He's an idiot that doesn't know he's an idiot. He thinks he's a genius, so he has an opinion about everything and God forbid if you should disagree with him. He's a butt. Don't hire him."

"I don't know what we're going to do. The superintendent has told us there's no one else available."

"That's nonsense," Sam said. "He just wants his person in there. Someone he can control. There's a guy I went to seminary with who's really sharp. He's down in North Carolina now, but wants to move back up here to be closer to family. I'll e-mail you his contact information. Have the search committee call him. I think he'd be a good fit."

They talked a bit more about Thanksgiving and Roger's girlfriend, whom Roger had met on an online dating service for Quakers, FindaFriend.com. Sam had visited the website once, in a moment of boredom, and after surveying the prospects had been greatly relieved to have already found his friend. They were mostly women who didn't shave their legs, ate organic food, went to vegetarian conferences, and shaved their heads bald so they would no longer be objectified by the dominant cultural understanding of female beauty. His brother had always dated causes, never people, which made for interesting family get-togethers. Vegetarians, libertarians, Tea Partiers, *Star Trek* junkies, dog rescuers, Second Amendment kooks, vegans, Roger dated them all, embracing their passion for as long as they were an item.

"So what's this girl like?" he asked his mother.

"She actually seems normal. She's a pediatrician. Very bright and personable. Pretty, too."

"Wow, I hope he doesn't blow it."

When Sam hung up the phone, he informed his wife they would be hosting Thanksgiving that year, and that his mother and father would be spending four days with them so they could attend worship and hear him preach.

"Did you ask them to get a hotel room?"

"I can't ask my parents that," Sam said. "It would hurt their feelings."

"I don't know where they're going to sleep. We don't have an extra bed. Plus, Levi will be home from college."

"Why don't we give them our bed and you can sleep on our couch? I'll sleep on the couch over at the office," Sam suggested.

"Oh no, you're not going to spend all your time over there and leave me to entertain *your* parents."

"They're your parents, too," Sam pointed out. "You call them Mom and Dad same as me."

"That doesn't mean they're actually my mom and dad. I have a mom and a dad. They live three hours from here and have the good manners not to impose themselves on us for four days without an invitation."

"Maybe we can buy one of those inflatable beds," Sam suggested.

So that's what they did, that very night. Drove to Costco and bought a queen-size inflatable bed and a set of sheets and two cheap, scratchy acrylic blankets, stiff as cardboard.

"Just to be clear," Barbara said, lest Sam had other ideas. "Your parents get the air mattress. If we make it too comfortable for them, they'll be here every weekend."

"Agreed," Sam said, alarmed at the thought of his parents visiting every weekend.

While Barbara got ready for bed, Sam phoned Doreen Newby to see how she was. Better, she said. She'd made a thorough search of their house and hadn't been able to find any incriminating evidence.

"I'm going through the garage tomorrow," she said. "And his workshop. If I don't find anything there, I guess I'll let him move back home. Anyway, Sam, I appreciate being able to talk with you today. I just had to talk to somebody."

"That's why I'm here. Happy to help. Like I told you this morning, I think Wayne made his decision many years ago, and it was to stay with you."

"I suppose you're right."

"Well, Doreen, get a good night's rest. Tomorrow's a new day, and I bet a much better day for you," he predicted.

"I'd appreciate it if you didn't tell anyone about our conversation," Doreen said.

"Of course not. It's no one's business but yours."

But he told Barbara. He'd always told her everything, just in case he got hit by a truck. Someone would have to take up where he'd left off. His not telling his wife all the church's secrets would have been like the president's not keeping the vice president in the loop. At least that's how Sam saw it. Someone would have to bring the next pastor up to speed. Might as well be Barbara. Besides, it was too interesting not to tell someone. Better to tell Barbara, who could keep a secret. Most of the time, anyway. Sometimes she told her mother, especially when someone did something scandalous. And sometimes her mother told her Sunday school class, but none of them knew anyone in Sam's congregation. At least that she knew of. Maybe a few people knew someone from Hope, but probably none of them knew anyone in the meeting. So Sam told Barbara all about Wayne's probably having had an affair with someone named Vicky but it had been a long time ago and it was probably over, though he couldn't be sure. But one thing Sam did know for sure was that what pastoral ministry lacked in pay, it made up for in intrigue.

12

Wayne Newby was released from the rehab center the day before Thanksgiving. Sam helped Doreen haul him home, then arranged Wayne in his recliner in front of the television, excused himself, and headed for Purdue to pick up Levi and bring him home. Levi was enjoying construction management and toying with the idea of adding a degree in architecture, except that Purdue didn't offer such a degree, so he was thinking of transferring to Ball State, which offered both construction management and architecture, and also happened to be the school attended by a certain girl he had met the week before.

"You'll like her, Dad. Her mother is a Methodist minister."

"I should have gone with the Methodists. Their ministers clean up."

"Yeah, but they have to move a lot. Monica has lived in four different towns."

"Is that her name? Monica?"

"Yep, that's her. Right now her mom pastors in the city, so Monica's coming over on Friday. Is that all right?"

"Sure," Sam said. "I look forward to meeting her. How did you meet one another?"

"Oh, some guys I hang out with went to high school with her. She came over from Ball State to visit them and we met then."

"I like Methodists," Sam said. "Most of them tithe, you know."

When they reached home, Sam's parents had arrived. A day early. Charles and Gloria Gardner removed from their car six large suitcases, blue plastic, that they'd purchased in 1971 for a trip to Milwaukee for a cousin's funeral.

"Help me carry these into your bedroom," Charlie Gardner said.

"Actually, we have an inflatable mattress for you and Mom. We're going to set you up in the living room," Sam said.

"That won't do," Sam's mother said. "Your father can't get up from one of those, not with his bad knees."

Levi offered them his bed.

"Oh, that will never do. We need at least a queen-size bed," Sam's father said. "I don't know how couples sleep on a full-size bed. I tell you what, Sam, you and Barbara take Levi's bed, your mother and I will take your bed, and Levi can sleep on the air mattress. Let's get these suitcases into your bedroom. Lend a hand here, Sam."

"I don't need an inflatable bed. I'll just sleep on the couch," Levi said.

Sam wondered if he and Barbara could return the air mattress and get their money back.

His parents began nosing around the house, opening doors and cabinets, inspecting.

"Nice place," his father said. "I like all the wood."

"How come you don't have any blinds on your windows?" his mother asked. "A neighbor could look right in and see you naked."

"There's a lot of privacy here," Sam pointed out. "The meeting owns ten acres. No one ever comes back here except for us."

"Have you met your neighbors?"

"Yes, we met them the first week we were here."

"Are they nice people? I heard people in the city can be dangerous," Charlie Gardner said.

"This isn't actually the city. It was a small town that's become a suburb. And we haven't met any thugs. Everyone has been very kind," Sam said.

Charlie Gardner gazed at the stone fireplace. "That's some kind of fireplace. I bet it puts out some heat."

"I suspect so. It hasn't been cold enough for a fire yet," Sam said.

"This is all so lovely," Gloria Gardner said, running her hand along the hickory cabinets.

"We really like it," Sam said.

Charlie Gardner peered out of the living room across the trees to the meetinghouse. "Show us the meetinghouse."

"Looks a lot like the house," Sam said. "Wood and stone and open space. Sure, let's go."

A brick path wound through the trees, connecting the parsonage to the meetinghouse. It had grown over, but Sam had spent a weekend pulling the grass from in between the cracks, then had borrowed a pressure washer from Wilson Roberts and blasted the bricks clean.

The meetinghouse was unlocked. Sam had taken to leaving it that way, not wishing to hike back to the house whenever he forgot his keys, which was about half the time. The idea of a locked church bothered him anyway. Leave it open. Someone might wander by in need of peace and quiet, in need of a soft place to sit and ponder and pray. He was pretty sure that if Jesus had a house he wouldn't lock it. So far no one in the meeting had complained. He'd thought Wanda and Leonard Fink would say something, but when he'd raised the subject in a monthly meeting, they had agreed without hesitation. "If someone wants in, they're going to get in," Leonard had said. "They'll just kick in a door or bust out a window. At least this way we'll save ourselves the expense of a busted door or window."

So Sam walked his parents right in and gave them the nickel tour.

"It doesn't smell like mildew, like our meetinghouse," Gloria Gardner said.

"Lots of glass in here," Charlie Gardner observed. "I bet you lose a lot of heat through those windows."

"Nope, if you notice, they're all southern exposure," Sam pointed out. "We actually gain heat in the winter. In the summer the sun is higher and doesn't shine through, so our air-conditioning costs are pretty reasonable."

"We spent ten thousand dollars heating our meetinghouse last winter," Charlie Gardner said.

"And it was still cold," Sam's mother said. "The Circle is knitting lap blankets for everyone to use."

His father talked at length about the furnace at Harmony Friends Meeting and how it hadn't worked right since Dale Hinshaw's son had first installed it twelve years before and how it was all the trustees could do to keep it running, but they didn't have the money to buy a new one so they really had no choice in the matter except to fix it and hope it didn't break down altogether. It exhausted Sam to listen to his father talk about it. That furnace had been the focus of hours-long meetings when Sam had pastored Harmony Friends, and now with his dad going on about it, it was still eating up his time.

"Sam doesn't want to hear about that dumb old furnace," Gloria Gardner said. "Stop talking about it."

"Worst furnace I've ever seen. Absolute piece of junk. The place that sold it to us is out of business. We can't even get parts for it anymore," Sam's father griped. "It'll probably blow up one day and kill the whole lot of us."

He paused and looked at Sam. "What kind of furnace you have here?"

"I have no idea."

"Don't you have to change the filters?"

"No. The trustees do that."

"Well, I'll be."

There had been a furnace committee at Harmony. Four men who gathered once a month and played poker in the furnace room of the meetinghouse basement.

"You don't have a furnace committee?" Charlie Gardner asked.

"Nope. We have a limb committee, a roof committee, and a pie committee, but no furnace committee."

"A pie committee? You have a pie committee?" Charlie Gardner asked.

"Yes, we do."

"Now that's a thought. I ought to mention that to our

church. We could use a pie committee," he said. "What exactly does a pie committee do?"

"Make pies," Sam said. "We have pie every Sunday after meeting for worship."

"Well, I'll be," Charlie Gardner marveled. "What will they think of next."

13

Sam and Barbara were in their bathroom, brushing their teeth and hissing at one another.

"What do you mean they're sleeping in our bed? I thought they were sleeping on the air mattress we just bought."

"My mom said my dad wouldn't be able to get up off an air mattress. Bad knees," Sam explained.

"Then let them have Levi's bed."

"Too small. They said they'd take our bed, we'd take Levi's, and Levi is sleeping on the couch."

"How long are they going to be here?"

"At least until Sunday after church," Sam said. "They haven't said anything about staying longer."

There was a knock on the door.

"We'll be right out," Sam called out.

"Hurry every chance you get," his father answered. "I can feel the old colon kicking in."

"There's a bathroom near the back door," Barbara said, her voice raised.

"I left my book in this bathroom. How much longer will you be?"

"There goes my nice relaxing bath," Barbara whispered to Sam. "They weren't supposed to be here until tomorrow."

Sam dearly loved his parents, but their talk of colons and weakened bladders and all manner of poorly functioning organs was starting to unsettle him.

They finished brushing their teeth, exited the bathroom, set up a bed for Levi on the couch, then padded off to his bedroom to sleep on his full-size mattress with a deep trough in the center that nearly reached the floor. Barbara set the alarm on her cell phone to sound at 5 a.m.

"Isn't that kind of early?" Sam asked.

"No, I have to start the turkey, and your father is going to want biscuits and gravy for breakfast."

"You don't have to make him biscuits and gravy," Sam said. "He can eat cereal."

"And he'll complain about it the rest of the day. It's just easier to make him the biscuits and gravy."

They discussed his parents a bit longer, grateful they now lived two hours away, which Sam thought was the perfect distance. Close enough for an emergency, but far enough away to avoid daily contact. They had both settled into sleep when the television set began to blare, awakening them. Sam leaped to his feet, threw open the bedroom door, and hurried down the hallway to the living room. His father was sitting in Sam's recliner and Levi was lying on the couch, a blanket over his head, his hands covering his ears.

"Dad, we're trying to sleep. Why don't you turn off the TV and go to bed?"

"Can't sleep. You know how it is. Strange bed and all. Thought I'd watch an old movie."

Sam sniffed the air.

"Have you been smoking?"

"It helps me relax," Charlie Gardner said.

"Dad, you cannot, under any circumstances, smoke in our home." Sam reached for the remote and clicked the television off. "You're keeping everyone up. We've all had a long day. If you can't sleep, why don't you go to your bedroom and read a little bit?"

His father snorted. "Can't smoke, can't watch TV. Might as well have stayed at a Holiday Inn."

Now there's an idea, Sam thought, but didn't say.

"We've had a long day, Dad, and need our rest," he repeated.

Charlie Gardner had not been like this when Sam was growing up. He had been thoughtful and nonsmoking and considerate of others, but retirement had changed him. He had become self-absorbed, obsessed with his own well-being, and dismissive of others. His mother had been phoning Sam regularly to complain.

"Your father...," she would begin.

"He was your husband before he was my father," Sam had taken to pointing out. "If you don't like how he's behaving, straighten him out."

Sam was beginning to understand why some adult children moved five states away. He couldn't imagine how bad it would be if he had continued to live in Harmony. He would have had to gas them.

His father tottered off to bed, and Sam did the same. He and Barbara lay awake, listening to his parents bicker, then heard his father get out of bed, open the door, and pass down the hallway to the thermostat. A moment later the furnace kicked on and ten minutes later Sam and Barbara were lying on top of their bed, their blankets kicked back, soaked with sweat.

"My Lord, this is awful," Barbara whispered to Sam. "I love your parents, but this is it. The next time they stay in a hotel. I don't care how much it hurts their feelings."

She sniffed the air.

"Did he smoke a cigarette?" she asked.

"Apparently."

"I am going to feed him so many biscuits and gravy tomorrow morning he strokes out at the kitchen table," she said.

Sam considered what his wife had just said. He was shocked at first, then saw the upside. "At least he'd die happy," he said.

14

Roger and his current girlfriend arrived an hour before mealtime the next day, just in time to help Barbara finish the meal and carry it to the table. Roger's girlfriend Christina rolled up her sleeves and went to work, endearing herself to the men, who admired a woman who knew her way around the kitchen, though they could never say that out loud, women being liberated and men having to value women for their intelligence. It wasn't like the old days.

Roger pulled Sam aside. "Quite a looker, don't you think?"

"Cuter than a button," Sam said. "How did you meet her?"

"Online. FindaFriend.com."

"Is she normal?"

"What do you mean, is she normal? Of course she's normal. Just look at her."

Sam looked at her, a bit too long in fact, and Barbara frowned at him. "Sam, why don't you and Roger set the table?"

"Sure, honey."

He and Roger spread out their grandmother's tablecloth and set out the family china and silverware their mother had hauled in for the event.

Christina and Barbara began carrying food into the dining room and setting it on the table.

"Christina, Roger said you met on FindAFriend.com. Are you a Quaker?" Sam asked.

"All my life," Christina said.

"What did you say your last name was? I know a lot of Quakers."

Christina laughed. She had a lovely laugh. Warm and real. "Yes, Quakerism is a small world. I hadn't mentioned it to your parents yet, because I wanted to see their faces when I told them, but my last name is Pringle. My father, Otis Pringle, is serving as their pastor at the Harmony Meeting."

"Oh, dear," Gloria Gardner said, smiling, but not putting her face into it. It looked more like she had just swallowed a fish bone at a dinner party and didn't want others to know it.

"You're that Christina?" Sam said. "I remember meeting you at one of the pastors' retreats years ago. And now you're dating my brother, you poor thing."

"I've heard my dad talk about your dad," Levi said. "He said…"

"I probably said how much I appreciate your father," Sam interrupted.

"Otis Pringle's daughter. Who would have guessed," Charlie Gardner said. "He mentioned he had a daughter named Christina, but I never put two and two together. And a doctor to boot. By the way, Christina, as long as you're here and we're talking medicine, I was wondering if you could take a look at my knees."

"What's wrong with your knees?"

"Christina didn't come here today to look at your knees," Sam's mother said. "You have a doctor. Don't pester Christina about your knees. It's her day off."

"She has to help me. She took a pledge to help sick people when she became a doctor."

"I did take a pledge, that's true, but knees aren't my specialty. I'm a pediatrician. If you were a child, it would be a different matter. If your current doctor is unable to help you, perhaps I could recommend an orthopedist."

The thought of paying a doctor was more than Charlie Gardner could bear. The chief appeal of Christina was that she was right there, was practically family, and likely wouldn't charge him.

"A knee's a knee. I think you'll do just fine. Why don't you just take a quick look at it."

Sam's father began unbuckling his belt just as Barbara entered the dining room, carrying the turkey. "What in the world are you doing? Pull your pants up!"

"Do you see what I have to live with?" Sam's mother said. "It's like this every day."

"It's no big deal. I just wanted to show her my knees."

"Some other time, Dad," Roger said. "It's time to eat."

"Maybe your knees hurt because you're overweight and don't exercise," Levi suggested.

"That's no way to talk to your grandpa," Charlie Gardner said.

"That's what I'd do if my knees hurt," Levi said. "Lose weight and exercise. It's just common sense."

"Time to eat," Sam said, attempting to head off a family squabble.

They took their places at the table, Sam at one end, his father at the other, Roger and Christina on one side, Levi, Gloria Gardner, and Barbara scrunched together on the other.

"Sam, honey, why don't you say grace. I just love to hear you pray," his mother said.

Everyone bowed their heads, and Sam began praying, thanking God for the food, remembering those who didn't have food, or clean water, or a place to live. It was a depressing prayer, which made them all feel guilty for what they were about to do—stuff themselves to the gills until they were so miserable they'd want to barf.

"And dear Lord, we ask you to watch over Addison while he serves our country. Please be with him and with all soldiers everywhere. Amen."

"I don't think you want God to be with all soldiers, do you?" Charlie Gardner commented. "You don't want God to be with the Taliban, do you?"

"Leave him alone. Sam, that was a beautiful prayer, and if God wants to be with the Taliban, that's His business, not ours," Gloria Gardner said.

Charlie Gardner was in no mood to drop the matter. "I don't hardly see why God would want to be with the Taliban. They don't even believe in our God. You can't go around lopping people's heads off and expect God to buddy up to you. That's all I'm saying."

"Honey, the turkey smells delicious," Sam said. "You've outdone yourself."

"Christina, what do you think of the Taliban?" Charlie Gardner asked.

"I've actually never met a member of the Taliban, so I'm probably not qualified to comment on them," she said diplomatically.

"I never met a Nazi, but I sure as heck wouldn't want to live next door to one," Charlie Gardner said.

"Speaking of living next door to someone, how are Harvey and Eunice Muldock doing?" Barbara asked, passing the sweet potatoes to Sam's father so he would fill his mouth and stop talking.

"They're fine," Gloria Gardner said. "Harvey had a hip replaced and Eunice had her uterus removed, but other than that, they're fine. Her uterus just plopped right out one day. In the dairy aisle at the Kroger."

"That's certainly good to know," Sam said.

"Christina, what do they call it when a women's uterus falls out?" Gloria Gardner asked.

"A prolapsed uterus."

"Enough about uteruses," Charlie Gardner said, turning to his wife. "We have news. Can I tell them now?"

"Go ahead," she said. "I know you're dying to."

"Tell us what?" Sam and Roger asked simultaneously.

Their father leaned back in his chair, set down his knife and fork, drew in a deep breath, beamed a happy smile of anticipation, then said, "Your mother and I have decided to move."

"Move? Where? To the assisted-living center in Cartersburg?"

"Oh my, no. Don't be silly," their mother said. "We're nowhere near needing that. That's for old people."

"I wouldn't live in one of those places if it was the last place on earth," Charlie Gardner said. "No, we've sold our house in Harmony and drove up yesterday and put earnest money down on a house right here in Hope. Right down the street, actually. We're gonna be your neighbors."

"Now I can hear you preach every Sunday," Gloria Gardner said, reaching over to pat Sam on his cheek. "I can't wait."

15

‿ᴗ

"Whoever said trouble came in threes couldn't count," Sam told Barbara that night, when it was just the two of them, squeezed into Levi's bed.

"I can't take this," Barbara said. "They'll be over here every day. We just became empty nesters, now we're going to have your parents camped out here day in and day out. We won't have any privacy."

Sam sighed. "Yeah, I wish they had talked with us before they did this."

They lay on their backs, staring up at the ceiling, thinking the worst.

"Don't get me wrong," Barbara said. "It's not that I don't love your parents. I do love them. It's just that they've become so, so..."

"Irritating," Sam filled in.

"Yes, and I know they don't mean to be. It's just that their world has grown so small, they think everyone's lives are like theirs. But we're busy. You have a job, I have a job, we have things we want to do, places we want to go."

"I know, I know."

"It's bad enough that we live in a parsonage and people call us and drop in at all hours of the day. I can put up with that. But I don't think I can do that and deal with your parents."

"You know, if my buddy from North Carolina moves up to pastor Harmony, maybe I can put in for his meeting?" Sam suggested.

"I don't want to move again. I like it here. I like my job. I'm making friends. Levi's here, and Addison will probably move here after he's out of the Army. Besides, now that Roger is dating Christina, don't you think it would be a little awkward if Harmony fired her father?"

"Yeah, I suppose."

Sam sighed.

"And just think, if Roger and Christina marry one another, I'll be related to Otis Pringle," Sam said.

"Technically, you won't be. Your brother will be. Let him worry about it."

"I can just see Otis Pringle coming to our house for Thanksgiving and Easter from now on," Sam said glumly.

On that happy note, they fell asleep. An unsettled, nightmarish sleep, in which Sam dreamed of falling and didn't wake up before he hit the ground with a splat.

It was still dark when Sam was nudged awake by his mother.

"What's wrong?"

"Nothing. We're just looking for the coffee. Can you tell me where it is?"

Sam sat up in bed, rubbing the sleep from his eyes. "What time is it, Mom?"

"Five a.m. We thought we'd get the coffee going."

Sam could hear his father singing "Moon River" in the kitchen.

"We keep the coffee in the refrigerator. The filters are in the cupboard above the coffeemaker."

Charlie Gardner poked his head in their bedroom. "Time to get up, sleepyheads."

"Dad, Barbara has the day off. We thought we'd sleep in."

"Oh, for crying out loud, you can sleep when you're dead. Climb on out of there and let's have some breakfast. What's for breakfast, Barbara? How about some biscuits and gravy?"

Forty-five minutes later they were seated around the kitchen table eating breakfast. Levi moved from the couch to his bed, dragging his blankets behind him.

"So, Dad, you and Mom have actually bought a house here?"

"You betcha. We got to thinking, you live here, Roger lives not far from here. Why should we be two hours away when all our family is here? Got a good deal when we sold the old place. Deena Morrison bought it. Didn't dicker over the price or anything. So here we are. Hope to be moved in by Christmas."

"I don't mean to pry," Sam said, treading carefully. "But with your age, do you think you should have bought a house? Now you'll have a lawn to mow and all that upkeep. Did you think about a condominium?"

"I have two strapping grandsons right down the street," his father said. "I figured they could mow the lawn."

Sam stared at him, incredulous. "Dad, I hate to rain on your parade, but you don't have two strapping grandsons right down the street. Addison is twelve hundred miles away in the Army and Levi's in college. They can't drop everything to take care of your house."

"And you're right down the street," Charlie Gardner continued. "I figured you could lend a hand with things. That reminds me, it's gonna need painting this spring. Think you could give me a week or two to help?"

"Sam's busy," Barbara said. "He works long hours, and so do I. We barely have time to keep our own place up."

"I tried telling him that," Gloria Gardner said. "I told him you had your own lives and we couldn't expect your help, but no, he had to get a house because he wanted a big garage and a place to put his tractor and his tools. Plus, he wanted a basement. What do we need with a basement at our ages?"

"You'll be glad for that basement when a tornado comes along," Sam's father said.

His parents commenced to squabbling, so Sam excused himself, showered, and went to his office to sleep on the couch, leaving Barbara to fend for herself.

16

At eleven o'clock Levi woke up and wandered into the kitchen. His mother was sitting at the table, a cup of coffee in hand, bleary-eyed.

"Don't forget that Monica's coming over for lunch," he said.

"Who's Monica?"

"My girlfriend. Well, not quite yet, but I'm working on it. Didn't Dad tell you? I invited her to lunch."

"You're going to have to un-invite her, or take her out to lunch. I honestly can't cook another meal."

"I don't have any money, or I would take her out to lunch."

"I'll give you money. You can take her to Bruno's."

"Where and what is Bruno's?" Levi asked.

"Just down the street from Riggle's Hardware, across the street from the library. Bruno is Italian, so you can get pizza."

Levi pondered her proposal, then nodded his head. "That can work."

"Then you can come back here for dessert. I'll make bread pudding."

"Ooh, did I hear someone mention bread pudding?" Charlie Gardner said, wandering into the kitchen. "What's for lunch? I'm famished."

"I was just telling Levi I'm not making lunch. You and Gloria can either fix yourself some leftovers or go out to eat."

Charles opened the refrigerator and peered inside, looking toward the back, opening the bins, inspecting the shelves.

"Hmm, might have to go out to eat," he said. He turned to Levi. "Did I hear you say you were going out to eat? Grandma and I will go with you."

"It's kind of a date," Levi said.

"Perfect, we'll make it a double date." He bellowed down the hallway, "Hurry up, Gloria. Levi's invited us on a double date with him and his girlfriend. Then we're coming back here for dessert. Barbara's making bread pudding."

Levi showered, then perched on the couch, looking out the window for Monica's car, which pulled in promptly on time.

"I already like that girl," Barbara said. "She's punctual."

"She's very precise. She wants to be an architect," Levi noted.

"Hey, she's a cutie," Charlie Gardner said, as Monica exited her car.

"Grandpa, I want you to be on your best behavior," Levi said. "I want her to like our family."

Before Monica could knock on the door, Levi had it open and was ushering Monica into the Gardner home.

"Charles," Gloria Gardner called from the back bedroom, "did you not change your underwear? I'm counting three pairs of clean underwear and there should only be two."

"There was no reason to put on a fresh pair. My old ones were just fine," he bellowed back.

Levi took Monica by the arm. "Introductions will have to wait," he said, smiling. "I've made reservations for us." And with that, he and Monica were out the door, in Monica's car, down the driveway, and gone from sight.

"Why did he do that?" Charlie Gardner asked. "Did he think we were going to drive ourselves?"

"I might be wrong, but I don't think Levi wanted Monica to hear you and Mom talk about your underwear," Barbara said. "That's just my hunch."

He retreated to the bedroom to tell Gloria their lunch plans had changed and Barbara made her escape, hurrying out the door and over to the office. Sam had the door locked and his office draperies closed.

"Let me in," she yelled, pounding on the door. "Quick, before your parents notice I'm gone."

She heard the lock click, then the door eased open and Sam pulled her in. "Did they see you leave?"

"I don't think so, and thank you, by the way, for sticking me with them all morning. They're your parents. You should be over there."

"I can't do it," Sam said. "I've tried. Really, I've tried. But I can't take it anymore. The snorting, the scratching, the farting. My Lord, it's unbearable."

"If we sneak out the back door of the meetinghouse, we can cut through the neighbors' yard and be at Bruno's in five minutes," Barbara said. "Levi's there with Monica."

"Let's do it," Sam said, and out they went, through the grove of trees, across their neighbors' backyard, out onto the street, a left at the corner and three blocks down to Bruno's, where they found Levi and Monica sitting at a booth in the corner.

Barbara reached across the table and shook Monica's hand. "I'm Barbara, Levi's mom."

"And I'm Sam, his dad."

"These are my parents," Levi said, miserably, his hopes of a romantic lunch dashed. He had taken a French class at Purdue and had memorized several phrases he had wished to try out on Monica, in hopes of winning her over. Perhaps break through Monica's love of precision and teach her there were other things worthy of her love. Like him, for instance. Still, maybe the lunch could be salvaged.

"I'm so hungry I could eat a frozen dog," Sam announced.

Levi's chances for love were fading by the minute.

They ordered two pizzas—vegetable for the women and meat for the men. Sam ordered himself and Barbara a bottle of wine. His parents would be at their house another forty-nine hours. They needed all the sustenance they could get. They peppered Monica with questions, trying at first to be casual. But after a while they dispensed with tact and asked about whether she liked being the daughter of a Methodist minister. Then Sam brought up the topic of pastoral pay and asked Monica how much Methodist ministers were paid these days, which turned out to be considerably more than Quaker ministers made, so Sam had another glass of wine to beat back his despair.

Bruno delivered the pizza to their table with a flourish. Sam and Bruno had become friends, despite Sam's initial fear that Bruno wanted him dead so he could run off with Barbara. But a few generous tips had caused Bruno to think well of him and now Bruno personally saw to Sam's meal whenever Sam stopped in to eat, which was fairly often. Bruno returned to their table halfway through their meal, introduced himself to Monica, held her hand, and asked if she was married.

"You Gardner men, you have beautiful women," Bruno said, kissing Monica's hand.

"To our beautiful women," Sam said, raising his wineglass.

He could never have drunk wine and toasted women in Harmony. The elders would have heard about it within the hour and he'd have been fired by suppertime.

"So, Monica," he said, feeling especially daring, "just how does one become a Methodist minister?"

17

Sam returned to the office feeling a bit woozy, three glasses of wine in him. It was the most alcohol he'd ever consumed at once and he fell twice walking home.

"Don't do that ever again," Barbara said, after his second fall. "You weren't meant to drink. There's a big bump on your head."

"Strange. I don't feel anything," Sam said.

"And you probably won't for another hour or two, then I suspect you'll be feeling a lot of things."

She made a pot of coffee at the meetinghouse and made him drink it, though he detested coffee. They sat on the office couch, wondering how long they could reasonably avoid his parents, who had been phoning the office every fifteen minutes. Sam had noticed their number on caller ID and hadn't answered. Then the phone rang and it was Jack Shear, Olive Charles's attorney, so Sam picked up the handset and said hello. They exchanged greetings and Jack cut to the chase.

"Regina Charles has upped the ante. She's suing for Olive's entire estate."

Sam was beginning to think God maybe didn't care for

Quakers. Methodist and Episcopalian churches could have large endowments, but God seemed to be hard at work keeping Quaker meetings modest and poor.

"And she's suing us for another million," Sam told him. "She claims she tripped on our sidewalk and hurt herself the day of Olive's funeral."

"When did you find that out?"

"Last week."

"Okay, Sam, you've got to let me know those things. It establishes a pattern that can influence a judge or jury on the estate settlement. Have you gotten any paperwork yet?"

"Not yet. Her lawyer stopped by the church to tell me."

"When you get the papers, give me a call, and I'll come by and get a copy. Who's her attorney?"

"Some bozo named Todd Cameron," Sam said.

Jack Shear snorted. "He's a crook. Gives all lawyers a bad name."

"Yeah, he seemed pretty slick."

"Don't talk to him if you can help it. Don't admit to anything. And if there's a deposition and you have to talk to him, let me know and I'll go with you. No charge for my services. I don't want to see all of Olive's hard-earned savings go to people like that."

"Thank you, Jack. I appreciate your help."

Sam had no sooner hung up the phone than it rang again. This time it was Doreen Newby calling to report she had found a girlie magazine in the bottom drawer of Wayne's workbench.

"It's time you did something about it," Doreen said.

"Doreen, that's your responsibility. I didn't find it. You did. If it bothers you, you need to be the one to talk with him."

"Oh, I talked with him. And he said a lot of men keep girlie magazines in their workbenches. I told him that was nonsense. You don't, do you?"

"Don't what?" Sam asked.

"Keep a girlie magazine in your workbench?"

"I don't even have a workbench," Sam said. "But if I did, I probably wouldn't keep a girlie magazine in it."

When he was a teenager, he had hidden a girlie magazine under his mattress. It had been passed through a succession of boys. By the time it had landed in Sam's hands, all but one of the pictures had been removed, which he had pointed out to his mother when she had discovered it, though it hadn't done any good, and he was sent for counseling to Pastor Taylor, who seemed even more embarrassed by the matter than Sam, and hemmed and hawed and talked about the reproductive cycle of the fruit fly and suggested to Sam's mother that she take him to his doctor, which she was all set to do until Sam's dad intervened and said, "For Pete's sake, Gloria, he's a boy. Ease up on him." And the matter was dropped, though every now and then Sam's mother reminded him of it and said how disappointed she was that he'd done such a thing.

Doreen Newby was starting to remind him of his mother.

"Just because Wayne had a girlie magazine in his workbench doesn't mean he doesn't love you," Sam said. "How old was the magazine?"

"August 1972."

"Then I think you should just forget about it."

"What kind of minister are you?"

"The best I know how to be. Doreen, you don't have to do what I'm telling you, but I think you'll be happier in the long run if you forgive Wayne and move forward with your marriage."

Doreen muttered something, Sam couldn't make it out, then hung up. It made him all the more grateful for Barbara, who, though she had grown feisty in her middle years, had never lost her basic kindness and good humor. Thinking about her, he felt guilty for letting her face his parents alone, so walked back together through the grove of trees to the parsonage, where he found his mother and father playing euchre at the kitchen table with Levi and Monica, while Barbara baked oatmeal raisin cookies. He had gotten chilled walking home, so decided to put their first fire in the fireplace. He opened the damper, gathered some kindling, carried in an armload of seasoned beech and hickory, and before long had a crisp fire crackling on the hearth.

"Grandpa, I see that extra card you dealt yourself," Levi said. "I can't believe you'd cheat your own grandson."

"He's a terrible fraud," Sam said. "He'd cheat Jesus at cards if he got the chance."

"I would never cheat," Charlie Gardner protested, even as a card slipped from his shirt sleeve.

Monica laughed. "You think that's bad? You should see my mom cheat at cards."

"I thought she was a minister," Gloria Gardner said.

"They're the worst kind of cheaters," Sam's father said. "No one ever suspects a minister of cheating, so they get away with murder."

"And just think, we might have three ministers in the family now," Gloria Gardner said, "Sam and Christina's father, Otis, and Monica's mom."

"There goes all the fun," Charlie Gardner said.

Gloria Gardner turned to Levi. "Just how serious are you and Monica? Do you think you two will get married?"

"Geez, Grandma, I don't know. We've only been on one date." His face was beet-red.

"I always thought I'd marry a Methodist," Monica said, smiling.

"Smart thinking," Barbara said. "Quaker husbands are a pain in the butt."

"You got that right," Gloria Gardner said.

18

That night Sam dreamed he was in court, being sued for a million dollars by Regina Charles, and the judge was on crutches, her leg broken from tripping on an uneven sidewalk. In his dream there were twelve jurors, all of them women with casts up to their hips, who stared daggers at Sam throughout the trial. They awarded Regina three million dollars and Sam had to sell everything he owned and work two extra jobs to pay off Regina so he wouldn't go to jail.

He woke up in a cold sweat, exhausted from his dream. It was five o'clock and he could hear his parents rattling around in the kitchen, making coffee. Two more days and they would be gone. Until they moved in down the street.

He had driven past the house the night before and walked around it. The houses on each side and across the street were immaculate, and Sam had to admit this house, too, had a certain charm despite its rough appearance. It was empty, the owners had moved, so he went up on the porch and peered through the windows and walked around back to see the yard, which was stacked with fallen limbs and old tires and three doghouses and a broken-down fence. This would be his future, he realized, serving at his father's beck and call, having to drop everything when his father phoned asking for his help.

"I just need you for a minute," he would tell Sam. "Won't take any time at all."

So Sam would hurry over, and still be there five hours later, balancing on a ladder, perhaps plummeting to his death.

There had been a five-gallon gas container behind the garage, half-full. Sam had entertained the idea of pouring the gas throughout the downstairs and torching the place. It would have saved him trouble in the long run, but he'd beaten back the temptation, returned home, gone to bed, and had nightmares instead.

Over breakfast Sam mentioned to his father that he had seen their new house.

"Pretty nice, eh?"

"Dad, I don't mean to be mean, but it's a mess."

"Nothing that a little elbow grease can't fix," Charlie Gardner said. "Besides, it was such a good deal, I couldn't pass it up. We can work on it together. It'll be a good father-son experience. We've never worked on a house together."

"There's a reason for that," Sam pointed out. "Neither one of us knows the first thing about remodeling."

"We can figure it out. It can't be all that hard. Maybe some of the guys in your new meeting can help us."

"Dad, they can barely stand upright. They're too old."

"Well, I'm not worried about it. It'll work out."

Charlie Gardner had spent his entire life worrying about things not likely to happen—an asteroid strike that would wipe out all humanity, the sun exploding, the end of gravity—

but had given little thought to things that were sure to occur, such as his retirement and how he would afford it.

Sam was beginning to suspect he was his father's retirement plan, that one day in the not-too-distant future his parents would show up on his doorstep, suitcases in hand, saying, "What's for dinner?"

"When were you and Mom planning to move?" Sam asked.

"Well, when we sold our house to Deena, we agreed to be out of it by Christmas, but Deena said if we needed to the New Year, that would be all right."

"Of course, there's a lot we have to do before the move," Gloria Gardner said. "There's the attic, the basement, the garage. We'll have to clean them out. Do you think you could borrow Uly Grant's truck and give us a hand?"

"I don't think it would take half a day," his father added.

Sam wanted to cry. His parents hadn't thrown anything away in the past forty years. Any effort to clean led to their stumbling upon some artifact from years past and reminiscing about the circumstances under which it had been acquired. His father had once spent three hours, upon discovering an old lawn mower blade, telling Sam about the first riding mower he'd ever owned, a 1957 Wheel Horse. He'd wept thinking about it, and spent the rest of the day polishing and sharpening the old blade, then hanging it in the living room, above the fireplace.

There was no way on God's green earth they would be ready to move by the New Year. Just as he was ready to point that out, the phone rang. It was Wayne Newby, calling to tell Sam he felt much better, and wanting to know if Sam could come over and help him down the stairs to his basement so he could check on his model trains.

"Has your family left?" Sam asked. "Doreen told me they were coming in for Thanksgiving."

"They're still here, but they don't think I should be on the stairs, so they're not gonna help me."

"Wayne, they know your situation much better than I do. If they don't want you using the basement stairs, I think you need to listen to them."

"Doreen's turned them against me. She found an old *Playboy* out in my workshop and told them all about it. I'd forgotten it was even out there. She says she's going to leave me unless I stand up in church and confess."

Oh, Lord. That was all Sam needed. A dirty old man standing in church, telling people he had drooled over a *Playboy* in 1972. One look at Doreen and people would maybe understand why he had done that in the first place. In any event Sam didn't want them dwelling on such things in meeting for worship.

"Tell Doreen that's not necessary. You've told me. That's enough. Now, about your basement, I think you need to listen to your family. At least until you get your cast removed. There's no sense in falling and breaking your hip."

What was it with people, anyway?

He promised to stop by the next week and help Wayne down the stairs. He excused himself and walked over to his office to work on his sermon. He had never liked preaching the Sunday after Thanksgiving. Everyone was gone, visiting or hosting relatives, it was not yet time to talk about Christmas, and people were sick and tired of being thankful. The past few years, he had taken that Sunday off and spent it at his in-laws' house, but he'd only been at Hope four months and didn't feel right asking for time off. Now he was stuck. Here it was, the day before Sunday, and he hadn't the foggiest notion what to preach about. He poked around through his stack of old sermons, looking for one he'd preached at Harmony. They'd never know. He found one he still believed, so dusted it off and tucked it in his Bible for Sunday morning, then walked to Riggle's Hardware to look at pocketknives.

19

He slept well Saturday night. Levi had returned to Purdue the evening before, so Sam's mom took the couch, his dad moved to Levi's bed, and Sam and Barbara were back in their own bed. Sam set their alarm clock for six, woke, showered, ironed a dress shirt and pants, then made his way over to the meetinghouse to copy the bulletin. It was still an hour before people would arrive, so he stretched out on his office couch for a nap. He was wakened by someone waggling his foot and opened his eyes to see Ellis and Miriam Hodge, from Harmony Friends Meeting, peering down at him.

"Up to your old habits, I see," said Ellis, laughing.

"What in the world are you two doing here?" Sam asked, rising to his feet and hugging them.

"We came up to Cousin Ruby's for Thanksgiving," Miriam said.

"You sure are getting adventurous," Sam said. "I thought after your trip to Gatlinburg you had sworn off travel."

"We decided to live on the edge," Ellis said. "Besides, have you ever tasted Ruby's pumpkin pie?"

"I have."

"Then you can see how a man might be tempted to drive a hundred miles for a piece."

"You could have come up with Mom and Dad. They've been here since Wednesday and are headed home this afternoon," Sam said. "Did you know they're moving?"

"Yes, they told us last week," Miriam said. "I still can't believe it. I never imagined your father would leave Harmony."

"It surprised us, too. But with us up here, and Roger in the city, they wanted to be closer to family."

As Sam spoke the words aloud, his parents' decision to move seemed to make a certain sense. They were getting older, after all, and wanted to be near their sons. But that house would be their undoing. Maybe it wasn't too late to steer them toward a condo.

They walked from Sam's office into the meeting room, which was beginning to fill with a surprisingly sizable crowd for the Sunday after Thanksgiving. When he'd arrived, back in August, meeting attendance had sat stagnant with a dozen or so elderly but stalwart Quakers. Sam took a quick head count. Thirty-some people, eight of them visitors, unrelated to anyone in the meeting. Sam greeted each one, and invited them all to stay afterward for pie and coffee. He was beginning to wish he'd spent a little more time on his sermon. He would have to dial up the delivery. Raise his voice a bit. Maybe throw in a story of a puppy. People liked puppy stories. He racked his brain, trying to think of a good puppy story.

They began with announcements, something Sam had been trying to eliminate since his arrival. Today they were mercifully brief, but one Sunday Wanda Fink had stood to announce the annual meetinghouse cleanup day and had chewed on the congregation for twenty minutes for letting things get shabby. Sam had had to shave ten minutes off his sermon that day, since Wilson Roberts stood at eleven thirty and headed to the kitchen for pie whether worship was over or not. It was his blood sugar, he'd explained to Sam. If he didn't have something to eat by eleven thirty, he would lapse into a coma and keel over.

Sam introduced his parents at the close of announcements, saying what a joy it was to have them visit and how pleased he was they were moving in just down the street and transferring their church membership to Hope Friends Meeting. He told a few more lies, Ruby Hopper introduced Miriam and Ellis Hodge, then Wayne Newby rose up on his crutches and said how nice it was to be back and thanked everyone for their prayers and people applauded.

Libby Woodrum, the local school principal and the first new attender on Sam's watch, volunteered to lead singing, so Sam welcomed her forward. It did nothing to improve their singing, but it was nice just the same and afterward Libby complimented them. Sam thanked her, she being Barbara's boss, and Sam wanting to stay on her good side to ensure his wife's continued employment. Libby's husband, Dan, had retired from his medical practice the year before and had already brought in six new attenders, all of them medical professionals up to their ears in money, some of which they had been dropping in the offering plate, a development members of the meeting found most intriguing.

Sam read the Scripture, then began his sermon. Five minutes in he noticed his father staring curiously at him, then leaning over to Sam's mother and whispering something in her ear. She nodded her head, as if in agreement. Charlie Gardner then elbowed Ellis Hodge, who was seated beside him. Ellis inclined toward Charlie, who again said something under his breath, all the while looking at Sam.

Sam moved forward with his message, trying to ignore his father, who was now tittering. Unnerved, Sam left out the puppy story and brought his sermon to an end, and they entered into silence. After a few minutes, Charlie Gardner rose to his feet. "I really enjoyed that message. I remember the Sunday that Sam gave it back in Harmony. I liked it then, too."

Ellis Hodge nodded his head vigorously. "Yes, I remember that sermon. It got Dale Hinshaw all worked up. I think you left out the part that got him upset, though. Boy, ol' Dale sure was mad that day!"

For as long as Quakerism had been around, well over 350 years, silence had been a central part of Quaker worship. People would listen for the voice of God, that still, small voice, then stand and share God's message. While Sam generally appreciated Quaker silence, today he wished it had never been invented. What had those early Quakers been thinking? Why hadn't it occurred to them that one day Charlie Gardner would use it as an opportunity to embarrass his son?

Sam stood and made his way to the pulpit, somewhat flustered.

"Let us stand for our final hymn," he announced.

"What about the offering?" Wilson Roberts called out. "You forgot the offering."

"Can't forget the offering," Charlie Gardner said, "or they won't be able to pay you."

"Could the ushers please come forward?" Sam asked.

"Oh my, it was my turn to get ushers and I completely forgot," Norma Withers said. "I'm so sorry." She appeared to be on the verge of tears. She had been forgetting so many things lately.

Dan and Libby Woodrum hurried forward. Sam bowed his head to pray, thanking God for first one thing and then another, asking God to be with the sick and the shut-ins, though with Olive Charles dead there were, technically speaking, no shut-ins left in their congregation.

He concluded with a tentative amen, only to hear his mother say, "I just love his prayers," and sigh contentedly.

Dan and Libby Woodrum collected the offering, then handed off the loot to Wilson Roberts, who hurried to Sam's office to count it, place it in an envelope, and fill out a deposit slip so he could drop it in the slot at the bank on his way home from meeting. His second month there, Sam had suggested they have two people count and deposit the money just to be on the safe side. Wilson had been so offended he hadn't spoken to Sam for an entire month. He had phoned Ruby Hopper after the elders' meeting at which it had been suggested.

"Well, I don't know, I don't see how I can keep on coming. He as much as called me a thief. Thirty years I've been a member of the meeting and not once has anyone questioned my counting the church's money. Then he comes along and all of a sudden I'm John Dillinger."

Ruby had talked him down and Sam had dropped the matter. Wilson stood in meeting for worship five weeks later and forgave Sam, though so far there was little indication he actually had.

They sang their last hymn, Norma Withers apologized once more for forgetting to line up the ushers, and Sam told her not to worry, then moved forward to give the closing prayer. As he neared the pulpit, Ruby Hopper raised her hand. "Sam,

I have been troubled by the lawsuit Olive Charles's niece has filed against the meeting. Could you please lift up this concern in prayer as we end our worship?"

"Who's suing us?" Norma Withers asked. "I wasn't aware we were being sued. Why would anyone sue us?"

"I'll explain it to you later," Hank Withers said, taking his wife by the hand.

Sam glanced at the clock. Eleven twenty-seven. He had three minutes before Wilson Roberts headed to the kitchen for pie. He launched into his prayer, thanking God for their time together, asking God to be with them in the week ahead, then, feeling a certain vigor, asking God to deal with Regina Charles, to soften her heart, so their meeting could move forward. "Lord, if it be Your will, we will gladly surrender this gift," he said, to dead silence. It was abundantly clear what the meeting felt the Lord should do. "But if it is Your will that we should have that money and use it for some great good, then we ask You to change Regina's heart." That earned him a few hearty *amens*.

He ended his prayer just as the clock struck the half hour. Wilson Roberts rose to his feet and lumbered into the kitchen for pie and coffee, a gaggle of Quakers in tow.

20

The Gardners, the Hodges, and Ruby Hopper went out to eat after meeting for worship. They spent ten minutes discussing where they might go before settling on the cafeteria, which pleased Sam to no end, he being a big fan of cafeterias.

"So what's this I hear about the meeting coming into a million dollars?" Ellis Hodge asked Sam in between bites on a chicken leg.

Sam glanced at Ruby. "Okay to talk about it?"

"I suppose so. Every Quaker meeting in a two-hundred-mile radius already knows about it."

Sam explained about the passing of Olive Charles, her bequest to the congregation, her niece's lawsuit—both of them—and the gift of Olive's house and 1979 Ford Granada.

"Never did care for the Ford Granada," Charlie Gardner said. "Terrible handling. Squishy on the corners."

"Ford makes a fine truck, but I've never really liked their cars," Ellis Hodge added.

"Why is Olive's niece suing you?" Sam's mother asked. "You didn't do anything to her. It's not like you own the church sidewalk."

"I guess it's customary. But I've been told the meeting's insurance policy protects me," Sam said. "So I'm not too worried."

This did nothing to allay his mother's fears. "They can't put you in jail, can they?"

"No, Mom, they can't put me in jail. Try not to worry."

"I read this story about this fella being sent to jail for some little thing and they forgot he was in there and he ended up being locked away for over twenty years," Charlie Gardner said. "I hope that doesn't happen to you."

"Oh, Lord. What if it did?" Gloria Gardner asked, panicked.

"Don't you think someone would notice I was gone? Don't you think Barbara would wonder where I was and say something to someone?"

"I don't know," Barbara said. "I might like the peace and quiet."

"Well, your mother and I would like to stay and visit," Charlie Gardner said, "but we have a long drive ahead of us so we better get going. Though if you don't mind, drive us past Olive's house."

Sam and Barbara hugged Miriam and Ellis good-bye and asked them to give their greetings to the folks at Harmony Meeting, which they promised to do the very next Sunday, provided they made it back to Harmony without someone running them off the road and killing them.

The Gardners wound through the side streets, coasting to a stop in front of Olive's house.

"Say, that's some house," Charlie Gardner said. "I wouldn't mind living there. What kind of shape is it in?"

"It looks fine to me, but it's hard to say. We won't know until we have it inspected," Sam said.

"I love that porch," Sam's mother said. "And look, Charlie, it has a carriage house behind it. You'd have room for all your tools."

"Kind of wish we had known it would be coming on the market," he said. "We've already gone and put earnest money down on the other house. Why didn't you tell us, Sam?"

"Probably because you didn't tell me you were moving."

"Still, it would have been nice if you had at least called and told us," his father said.

"Dad, I don't look at every house for sale and think to myself that I better call and tell you about it."

"I have the feeling you don't want us to move up here," his mother said.

"Oh no, Mom. Not at all. I think it will be nice to have you closer," Sam said, trying his utmost to sound sincere. He did love his parents, after all, though he had discovered it was easier to love them when they lived two hours away.

"What's the meeting going to do with that house?" Charlie Gardner asked.

"I don't know for sure," Sam said. "We have to wait for Olive's estate to get settled first. It might go to her niece. But if we do get it, I suspect we'll sell it. We don't want to have to take care of it."

"Maybe you could make your mother and I a deal."

"That wouldn't be right," said Sam. "Besides, I'm sure we'd have it appraised and try to get what it was worth."

"Kind of wish we hadn't put down earnest money on that other house," he said again, more wistfully this time. "Just wish you had been thinking ahead a little bit, Sam."

Sam turned onto the meetinghouse street, praying his parents' car would start, and that nothing would prevent their quick and safe return to Harmony.

Charlie and Gloria Gardner pulled out of the driveway at 3 p.m., and by 3:05 Sam was on the couch, asleep. At 3:15 their phone rang. It was Norma Withers, calling to apologize for the third time.

"I don't know what's wrong with me. I've been forgetting everything lately."

"Hank told me about your Alzheimer's. Your forgetfulness might be related to that."

Norma began to weep. "I told him not to tell anyone."

"Actually, you told him he could tell me," Sam said. "But I haven't told anyone else."

Except for his wife, of course, and perhaps he had mentioned it to Wayne Newby when Wayne had complained about his broken leg. Yes, he was sure of it now. Wayne had been moaning and griping and Sam had said it could have been worse, that Wayne could have had Alzheimer's like Norma Withers. Then Sam had remembered he wasn't supposed to tell anyone except Barbara, so he'd made Wayne promise not to tell anyone except for Doreen. Besides them, no one else knew. Ruby Hopper knew, of course, but that was it. Sam, Barbara, Wayne, Doreen, and Ruby. Other than that it was a secret.

"I don't remember telling Hank he could tell you," Norma said.

"Yes, he told me you gave him permission to tell me, since I'm your pastor. In time you'll want to let others know, but you should decide how and when to do that. Until then your secret is safe with me."

"Thank you, Sam. I can't stand the thought of other people knowing. They'll start treating me differently and I don't want that."

"I understand."

They talked a bit longer, then Sam phoned Wayne and Doreen and reminded them not to tell anyone.

"Wish you had reminded me this morning before I told Dan and Libby Woodrum. I felt they needed to know," Wayne said.

"Oh, for crying out loud. I told you not to tell anyone. Norma doesn't want people knowing."

"It's not like the Woodrums are going to blab it all over town. Besides, I felt they needed to know, her being a school principal and all."

"What's being a principal got to do with it?"

"Well, they're used to knowing private stuff about people and I just thought she should know," Wayne said.

"Don't tell anyone else. Norma wants to tell people herself, when she feels ready. If she tells you, act surprised."

"Of course I will. I'm not stupid, you know."

Sam didn't respond.

Sam said good-bye, then lay back down on the couch, stewing. He never should have told Wayne and Doreen, who, it appeared, were incapable of keeping a secret.

21

Sam arrived at his office early the next morning, having fallen behind in his work during his parents' visit. He sketched out his sermons for the upcoming Christmas season, and wrote a devotional for the congregational newsletter, a three-hundred-word essay on the importance of trust and not violating confidences. He ate lunch at his desk, a peanut-butter-and-bacon sandwich warmed in the microwave, and was just stretching out on the office couch for a nap when the telephone rang. He picked it up on the second ring.

"Hope Friends Meeting. This is Sam Gardner, the pastor."

"Hi, Sam. Jack Shear here."

Olive's lawyer. This could be interesting.

"I have some news for you."

"Good news or bad news?" Sam asked.

"I guess it depends on how you look at it."

"What is it?"

"Olive's niece, Regina, died suddenly yesterday. I just got word from her attorney."

"That's horrible. What happened?"

"She was hit by lightning."

"Oh my. When did this happen?"

"According to her attorney, at exactly eleven twenty-nine a.m. yesterday. She was walking into a Walmart and was struck by lightning. A freak thing. It was sprinkling, and *boom!* Stopped her heart and her watch. That's how we know the precise time. Anyway, she had her attorney's business card in her pocket, so the police called him and he called me."

"Oh, that poor woman," Sam said. "How sad."

"Her attorney wants to know if you could do her funeral?"

"Sure, I guess so."

"That's the bad news, the good news is that she's no longer suing you or the church. The lawsuit ends with her death. She has no family to carry the suit forward."

Sam thought for a moment. "I'm glad the suit is over, but I sure didn't want it to happen this way."

"One more thing," Jack Shear said. "With no family, her attorney is making her funeral arrangements. He wants to know if her funeral can be held at the meetinghouse."

"Yeah, that's not a problem."

"And her lawyer said she's being cremated. He wants to know if her ashes could be sprinkled in Olive's backyard. She had mentioned staying at Olive's as a little girl and playing in the backyard. The lawyer said the house was really all she wanted. They were asking for more in hopes of being able to settle for the house."

"I wish they had told us that. Maybe we could have reached an agreement," Sam said, starting to remember he had argued against giving her anything and feeling guilty.

"Apparently Regina's parents were alcoholics. Died young. So Regina ended up spending a lot of time with her aunt Olive as a little girl. Then she started into drugs when she was a teenager and things went downhill from there. Olive tried, but couldn't save her."

"How tragic," Sam said. "Yes, we'll be happy to have Regina's funeral at the meetinghouse, and I'll make sure her ashes get spread in Olive's backyard. It's the least we can do."

Neither one spoke for a moment.

"A tragic ending to a tragic life," Jack Shear observed.

"When you talk with Regina's attorney, give him my telephone number and tell him to call me when he's ready to make funeral arrangements. Meanwhile, I'll let the folks here know what's going on."

They traded good-byes and Sam hung up, then picked up the phone again to call Barbara with the news.

"What time did you say she died?" Barbara asked.

"Eleven twenty-nine on Sunday morning, according to her watch."

"That's kind of creepy when you think about it."

"What do you mean?"

"Don't you remember? Ruby asked you to pray about the lawsuit at the end of worship, so you asked God to change Regina's heart. Do you remember doing that?"

"Kind of." Sam had never been good at remembering to pray, and when he did, he wasn't adept at remembering what he had prayed for.

"When you were praying, I looked at the clock and it was eleven twenty-eight. Then a minute later, Regina gets hit by lightning and dies. Looks like God changed her heart all right."

"Oh, I don't believe that. It was just a coincidence," Sam said. "God doesn't kill people."

"Don't you think it's just a little odd, though?"

"Well, sure," Sam said. "It's very odd. But it's just a fluke."

"Remind me never to get on your bad side," Barbara said.

"Stop that."

"One minute you're praying for God to do something about the lawsuit, the next minute the person suing us is struck by lightning. I didn't know you had that kind of pull."

"I'm hanging up," Sam said. "You're a sick individual."

He composed an e-mail to the members and attenders, informing them of Regina's demise and the lawsuit's dismissal, read it over several times, changed a word or two, then sent it out.

Sam sat at his desk thinking. During the long course of his ministry, he had often asked God to intervene in situations and had usually been disappointed. He had prayed for Dale Hinshaw to change churches and Fern Hampton to move to Florida, but they'd both stayed put. Then, almost casually, he had suggested to God that he might do something about a lawsuit and *bam!* just like that, Regina Charles was a smoking heap of charred flesh in a Walmart parking lot. But God wouldn't do that, would he?

Sam was slightly peeved. He had spent most of his adult life developing his theology, only to have it upended by a bolt of lightning. That was the problem with religion. You no sooner made up your mind about something than you had to change it.

22

The fight began the next day, with an e-mail from Wanda Fink praising the Lord for intervening in their lawsuit, opening the way for Hope Friends Meeting to receive a million dollars, which she believed should be sent to her nephew, a missionary in Norway, who at that very moment was risking life and limb to preach the gospel to socialists.

Five minutes later Hank Withers responded, suggesting a fellowship hall and new kitchen for the meetinghouse. He attached an architectural rendering, and pointed out to Wanda that if her nephew wanted to live in Norway, that was his business, not the meeting's. Wayne Newby joined the battle, reminding everyone the meetinghouse roof needed replacing.

"Especially since you destroyed it trying to cheat our insurance company," Wanda Fink responded, hitting *Reply to All*.

Sam let them rage on, hoping they would wear themselves out, but they showed no signs of fading, so he chimed in after a few hours, pointing out the money wasn't theirs yet, and there was no use getting worked up about something that hadn't yet happened.

"At some point," he added, "we might want to give prayerful consideration to hiring a church secretary, freeing me up to do ministry instead of office work."

"I've worked in an office for twenty-three years," Wanda Fink responded in capital letters and bold print, "and I'd like to think it was ministry. And I would appreciate it if my pastor understood that and acknowledged my ministry instead of acting as if he is the only one who has ever ministered to others."

Sam turned off his computer.

He phoned Levi at Purdue to see how his classes were going and to nose around in his private business, asking how Monica was and whether they were still dating since she had met his family.

Monica was fine; yes, they were still dating, but he preferred not to talk about it.

"Have you heard from Addison?" Levi asked, changing the subject.

"Last night," Sam said. "He called."

"How's he doing?"

"He sounded good. He wanted to know if we could come see him. He has a long weekend in two weeks."

"Are you going?"

"No, Mom can't get off work, and it costs too much. Airline tickets, rental car, hotel room. We don't have that kind of money."

"I miss him," Levi said. "I wish he had come up here to school. We could have shared an apartment."

It killed Sam to think of his son being so far from home. Or worse yet, being sent overseas, which was a distinct possibility and one Sam didn't want to think about—his son in

Afghanistan or South Korea and someone doing something stupid and a war erupting and his little boy in the thick of it. He had spent considerable time praying Addison's arches would fall and he would be discharged.

He and Barbara wrote Addison that evening, as they did every week, filling him in on the news, trying not to let their worry for him seep into the letter. It was hard to know the tone to take. If their letter seemed too happy, Addison would think they didn't miss him. But if their letter betrayed their anxiety, he might feel guilty for moving away. So they wrote about their jobs and the grandparents and stupid things people had done. Occasionally Addison wrote back, not as often as they would have liked, but then he had never been one for writing. He had met a young Mormon lady in the army who was studying to be a medic. He had attended church services with her and was thinking of joining the Mormon church, which intrigued Sam.

"Don't they wear special underwear?" he'd asked Barbara after reading the letter.

"How would I know what kind of underwear they wear? I don't ask Mormons to show me their underwear."

They Googled the phrase "Mormon underwear" and sure enough, they did. Except they were called *temple garments*. They looked like something Gabby Hayes might wear prospecting for gold.

"I can't see Addison wearing those," Barbara said.

"There's no telling what a man in love will do."

They discussed underwear a bit longer. Sam had been a briefs man all his life, but had recently switched to boxers and had found the change exhilarating, mentioning it to Barbara several times a day. She worried that was what their life with the children gone would become. A discussion of underwear. Some couples, she knew for a fact, discussed lofty ideas. Not them.

"It says here the temple garment, and I quote, 'strengthens the wearer to resist temptation, fend off evil influences, and stand firmly for the right.'"

"Where are you reading that?" Barbara asked.

"Wikipedia. A man named Carlos Asay said that."

"Who, pray tell, is Carlos Asay?"

"Not is, was. He's dead. He was a Mormon bigwig," Sam said.

He read on.

"That must be some powerful underwear to resist temptation, fend off evil, and stand firmly for the right."

On the one hand, conversations with Sam could be tiring. On the other hand, he was a whiz at trivia games.

"Don't you think that's a little weird?" Barbara asked.

"No more weird than old-time Quakers not having lapels on their jackets or buttons on their clothes," Sam said.

"Or believing God created the world in six days, five thousand years ago," Barbara added.

"There you go."

"Do you think we'll ever go to Paris?" Barbara asked.

"What brought that up?"

"We're sitting here talking about underwear. I just want to know if our lives are going to get any more interesting."

"Do you want to go to Paris?" Sam asked.

"Yes. I want us to save our money and go to Paris, so that when I'm old and in a nursing home, I don't have to say, 'I wish I had seen Paris just once.'"

"Then we'll save our money and visit Paris," Sam said.

"Besides, I've always wanted to see a French hardware store."

The matter settled, they shared a bowl of ice cream and went to bed, where Sam whispered French-sounding words in Barbara's ear until she gave in to his endearing charms.

23

Sam heard the mail truck before he saw it, putt-putting down the meetinghouse lane. He had struck up a friendship with the mailman, so they chatted a few moments, then the mailman handed Sam the mail a piece at a time, reading the name of each sender aloud.

"Junk mail, junk mail, electric bill, cancer society, a letter from a church in North Carolina, college fund-raising letter—"

Sam was studying the letter from the North Carolina church. It was one of the Quaker meetings he'd applied to the year before after being fired from Harmony Friends Meeting.

"What's it say?" the mailman asked.

"I didn't think mailmen were supposed to be so nosy."

"Are you kidding? That's the best thing about being a mailman, seeing what people get for mail. You know Wayne Newby?"

"Yes, he's a member of this church."

"He subscribes to *Playboy*, but doesn't want his wife to know. He tips me five bucks if I deliver it straight to him without his wife seeing it."

Sam liked secrets as much as the next pastor, but he could have gone a long time without knowing Wayne Newby still read *Playboy.*

"I didn't think mailmen were supposed to tell what they delivered to other people. Isn't that part of your oath?"

"You mean 'Neither snow nor rain nor heat nor gloom of night stays these couriers from the swift completion of their appointed rounds'?"

"Yeah, that's the one," Sam said. "Didn't you swear to do that?"

"Not me, I'm a union man. We don't have to swear to anything. Besides, it doesn't say anything about reading people's mail. So what's your letter say?"

"I'd rather not say. If I tell you, you'll tell Wayne Newby."

"I promise I won't."

"Did you promise Wayne Newby you wouldn't tell anyone he subscribed to *Playboy?*" Sam asked.

"Maybe I did."

"Well, there you go. This is one letter I prefer to keep to myself."

"Is it a job offer?"

"Not saying," Sam said.

"Did someone die?"

"Not saying."

"If someone gave me a job offer in North Carolina, I'd jump on it with both feet. It's beautiful down there. Warm, too. You can golf in February."

"I don't golf," Sam said. "Now stop being nosy and go deliver the rest of your mail."

It was a job offer. Well, not quite an offer, but an invitation to visit their meeting and interview for the job of senior pastor. From one of the largest Quaker meetings in America. Five hundred members, 425 of whom were in worship every Sunday. A salary of close to one hundred thousand dollars, free housing, health insurance, and a retirement package to boot. The letter didn't mention that, of course, but Sam had heard it from Scott Wagoner, his friend from seminary, who was plugged in, with a capital P.

He waited until after supper to tell Barbara, sliding the letter across the kitchen table, not saying anything, watching her reaction as she read it.

"What are you going to do?" she asked.

"I don't know. I kind of wish they had contacted me last year when I was looking for a meeting. It doesn't feel right to leave here after only five months. Feels like I'd be jumping ship to make more money."

"People do it all the time," Barbara pointed out.

"It's a little different when you're a pastor. I told Hope Meeting I felt called to be here. Now what will I tell them? That after five months I feel called to go somewhere else that just so happens to pay four times as much money?"

"They don't need to know what you're being offered."

"Besides, I'm kind of curious to know what Hope Meeting will do with the million dollars we're getting."

The letter lay on the table between them, one more interesting addition to their lives. Their sons' flying the coop, Olive Charles's bequest to the meeting, Wayne Newby's fascination with naked women, Norma Withers's being afflicted with Alzheimer's, his parents' moving in down the street, his brother Roger's romancing Otis Pringle's daughter, Levi's dating a Methodist, the lightning-quick death of Regina Charles, Addison's dabbling in Mormonism, a possible trip to Paris, maybe, sometime, and now this, a job offer out of the blue. Sam had labored his entire life to avoid drama and decisions, only to be assailed by them at every turn.

"I'll pray about it," he promised Barbara.

"So in other words, you're not taking it."

"I didn't say that."

"Sam Gardner, we've been married thirty years. I know you better than you know yourself. When you say you're going to pray about something, it means there's no way you're going to do whatever it is you're praying about."

"Just being careful, that's all."

"Have you thought any more about Paris?" Barbara asked.

"I'm praying about that, too."

"Oh, for Pete's sake. We'll never go anywhere. North Carolina, Paris. We're going to stay in Indiana our entire lives, aren't we?"

"I thought you liked your new job and didn't want to move," Sam said.

"That was before a Quaker meeting offered you a hundred thousand dollars."

Their telephone rang, quieting their disagreement.

It was Levi, calling from college, asking if Sam could transfer some money into his checking account.

"I can't. I promised your mom I would save our money for a trip to Paris. Why do you ask? Did you need something?"

"I wanted to buy Monica something for Christmas," Levi said.

"But if your mom and I pay for it, then it will be us buying Monica something for Christmas, not you," Sam explained. "I'm sure she would prefer something from you, however modest. Besides, it's four weeks until Christmas. That's plenty of time to come up with the money you'll need."

"I was afraid you'd say that."

"Isn't it nice to have a predictable father who never surprises you?" Sam said. "You never have to worry that I'll be erratic, and therefore prone to volatile outbursts."

Barbara rolled her eyes.

"But I'll tell you what I'll do," Sam said. "If you want to make Monica something in my workshop, I'll lend you a hand. Maybe a birdhouse or a cutting board."

"If she has a clothesline, I can help him make her a clothespin bag that hangs on the line," Barbara said.

"Did you hear that? Your mother offered to help you make her a clothespin bag. And I could help you make her a set of clothesline poles."

Levi, unfortunately, had hung up, unaware of his parents' generosity.

24

The elders' meeting was that night and the disagreement over Olive's estate that had been smoldering on the back burner was moved to the front and burst into flames.

It began innocently enough, when Hank Withers asked Sam if Olive's attorney had mentioned when they might receive the money.

"You can't spend it fast enough, can you?" Wanda Fink snarled.

It was, in fact, a genuine snarl. Her upper lip was raised, revealing her incisors, which were unusually pointy and menacing.

Norma Withers smiled pleasantly. She had been doing a lot of that lately. Staring at people and smiling.

"What's so funny?" Wanda Fink snapped.

"You have the prettiest teeth," Norma said. "I've never really noticed them before."

"Are you mocking me?"

The others fell silent, studying the table.

Sam suggested they enter into silent worship, hoping the

anger might dissipate, but certain of them seemed perfectly content to be angry and the brawl escalated.

"I would appreciate it if you didn't talk to my wife in that tone of voice," Hank Withers said.

"I would appreciate it if you didn't spend all the church's money on an addition we don't need," Wanda Fink shot right back, as if she had loaded the line and had been waiting for the first chance to fire it. "There are less than twenty people in this church. We have all the room we need."

"This church needs to get serious about its mission," Leonard Fink said. "There are people in this church who don't even know what it means to be saved. How come you never preach about that, Sam?"

It was the first time Sam had heard Leonard Fink speak in a church meeting. Mostly he just nodded whenever his wife said anything. Sam liked it better when Leonard nodded.

"Sam's preaching is good enough for me," Wayne Newby said.

Sam took little comfort in being defended by the church's resident playboy, but he thanked Wayne just the same.

"I liked the message you gave last Sunday," Norma Withers said. "It was very nice."

"Yeah, and that was some prayer you gave, too," Wayne added. "You ask God to do something about the lawsuit and the next thing you know Regina Charles is dead as a mackerel." He glanced at Wanda and Leonard Fink and said, "You might keep that in mind and try to stay on Sam's good side."

"This conversation isn't serving any purpose," Ruby Hopper said, struggling mightily to keep the elders on track. "We need to give serious, prayerful thought to how best to use this gift we've been given. Let's stay focused, please, and treat one another with respect."

They sat silently for a few moments, calming themselves.

"I certainly don't mean to diminish the importance of spirituality," Hank Withers said cautiously, in a lowered voice, "but we've always intended to add on to the meetinghouse, we've just never had the money. Now we've been given a way to do it."

"And what about my nephew?" Wanda Fink asked. "He gave up a good job to move his family to Norway so he could preach the gospel and no one is helping him, not even his own church."

"I don't see why that should be our responsibility," Hank said. "We didn't send him. If his own church won't support his ministry, there might be a good reason. Maybe they know something we don't."

"Poor planning on his part does not constitute an emergency on our part," Wayne Newby added. "It says that in the Bible."

"You don't even read the Bible," Wanda said. "If you did, you'd know the Bible says no such thing."

"I read the Bible," Wayne protested. "I can even quote it. 'Your two breasts are like two fawns, twins of a gazelle, that feed among the lilies.' Song of Solomon, chapter four, verse five. You can look it up yourself."

Wayne had memorized that verse at the age of fifteen, at church camp, where he had been sent home early for saying it when the camp counselor asked him his favorite Scripture. He had heard many Bible verses since, none of which he remembered, but that one had lodged in his mind. He thought of it at various times, mostly when he looked at *Playboy*.

"Hank read that verse to me the night of our honeymoon," Norma Withers added. She sighed wistfully, lost in the memory.

"Let's move on," Hank said quickly. "Ruby, what else is on our agenda?"

They talked another hour about various things, but their minds weren't in it for thinking of Hank and Norma and their honeymoon night.

Walking home, Sam thought it had been a fairly typical church meeting: a few hot sparks, much meandering, little focus, a snatch of gossip, a misquote or two from the Bible, and finally a decision to hold another meeting.

He thought more about the Quaker meeting in North Carolina. It was located next door to a Quaker college and full of professors. He wondered what their elders' meetings were like. He bet they didn't argue over chicken-and-noodle dinners and whether or not the toilets needed replacing and how to cheat the insurance company into paying for a new roof. He bet they just said, "Sam, that's why we pay you. You make the decisions." He'd never been told that in any church he'd ever pastored. Just once, it would be nice.

"Sam, we don't need to have a committee meeting to select a new hymnal. You just pick it out, let us know how much they cost, and we'll cut you a check for them."

"Sam, we're going to give you a credit card to cover your expenses. You don't need to get a committee's permission for every little thing you get for the church."

"Sam, you don't need to ask our permission to take a day off. If you need a day off, take it off. We don't need to know your schedule."

He thought maybe the Quaker meeting in North Carolina

would say those kinds of things. They were professionals, after all, busy people who didn't have time to bicker about little things like hymnals or gas money or dentist appointments. People who could spend a million dollars at the drop of a hat, then eat a piece of pie and not give it a second thought.

Maybe Barbara was right. What would it hurt to talk with them?

25

He read the letter from the Quaker meeting in North Carolina once more, called the name and number at the bottom of the page, and introduced himself to the woman who answered the phone.

"Who did you say this was?" she asked.

"Sam Gardner. You sent me a letter inviting me to apply to be your pastor. I'm phoning to thank you for the invitation, but I just started here and feel I should stay."

"That's okay," she said. "We sent the letter to every pastor currently serving a Quaker meeting."

That took a little shine off the apple.

"Well, I just wanted you to know I wouldn't be applying."

"Okay. Thanks for calling. What did you say your name was again?"

"Sam Gardner."

"Okay. Thank you."

She didn't ask him to pray about it, or give it a few days' thought, or at least meet with them once to hear what they had to say.

He went upstairs to help Barbara fold the laundry.

"How'd they take it?" she asked.

"Oh, they were disappointed, but they understood," Sam said.

"It's probably for the best," Barbara said. "Our parents are here. Levi is here. I like my new job."

"That's what I was thinking, too."

Sam lay awake that night, worrying. If Hope Friends ever gave him the boot, he'd be in trouble. He'd read an article on the Internet about how people in their fifties were at their peak earning potential. In upper management with retirement in sight. So much for that. A college degree in theology. What had he been thinking?

He slept in the next morning, then showered, ate breakfast, and walked the four blocks to Hank and Norma Withers's house. They had been after him to visit, so he carved out the entire morning, thinking they might want to discuss Norma's Alzheimer's. They sat at the kitchen table, drinking coffee, which Sam couldn't stand no matter how much sugar he added.

"Sam, we need you on our side on this building addition," Hank said, not bothering to ease into the conversation.

"Who's 'we'? What side are we on?"

"Wayne Newby, Wilson Roberts, Dan Woodrum, and me. We're all in agreement. If Wanda and Leonard get their hands on this money for their nephew, we'll not have anything to show for it. They did this exact same thing about five years ago. Wilson Roberts donated twenty thousand dollars to the meeting and Wanda pitched a fit until we sent it to some missionary down in Bermuda. She's not going to stop until she gets her way with this money, too."

"Perhaps we can do both things," Sam suggested. "Build an addition onto the meetinghouse, and offer some financial assistance to her nephew's ministry."

"Nope, won't work," Hank said. "I've been running the numbers. The addition will come in a little above a million. It's going to take all the gift and more. Norma and I are willing to foot the difference, unless the meeting gives money to Wanda's nephew, then we won't give anything. It's all or nothing."

So much for a raise, Sam thought.

"Are you with us?" Hank asked. "Because I have to tell you, Sam, if this doesn't happen, there'll be people leaving the meeting, including us. We're tired of twiddling our thumbs, never moving forward."

Sam's gut clinched. The if-we-don't-get-our-way-we're-leaving threat. He was surprised it was coming from Hank, who up until then had seemed reasonable. *He must really dislike Wanda Fink*, Sam thought.

"I understand your frustration," Sam said. "But as the pastor it isn't appropriate for me to take sides. I love everyone involved." That was a slight exaggeration, but one he could live with.

"You're a good pastor," Norma Withers said, smiling, taking Sam by the hand. "We're lucky to have found you."

Sam wished more people in his congregation had Alzheimer's.

"Sam, you need to know that one of the reasons we hired you was that you seemed like a go-getter to us. Someone who could get us moving."

Sam couldn't imagine what might have given them that impression, but was flattered nonetheless.

It was a perfect moment for a cliché.

"I do want to see the meeting move forward, Hank. But it will take all of us, working together."

"You're such a wise pastor," Norma said.

It was all Sam could do not to agree. He did feel especially wise. He was beginning to think the world of Norma Withers.

"Hank, let's work our way through this. We don't even have the money yet. No telling when we'll get it. Though I can't choose sides, and don't even want to think in terms of sides, I can assure you that your concerns will be taken seriously."

Hank nodded, somewhat mollified.

"Perhaps you and Wilson and Wayne could make some kind of presentation to the meeting so the rest of us can understand it a bit better," Sam said. "Ask Dan Woodrum to help you. Let's help him feel included."

"We can do that."

"Try not to use all the money," Sam added. "I've heard others say we shouldn't spend all that money on ourselves, so you might find a way to leave some money on the table for other causes."

Like a raise for your pastor, for instance, Sam thought, but didn't say.

"I guess it's like any other project. It's what you want versus what you can afford," Hank conceded.

"Yes, that's right."

Sam stayed a bit longer, discussing Norma's Alzheimer's and how she felt and what they were going to do. Not much they could do. Take some pills, do crossword puzzles, beat it back a few years, hope for a miracle.

"Then after a while she'll forget my name and that I'm

her husband and she'll wonder who that strange man is who comes to see her every day in the nursing home," Hank said.

Norma smiled.

Hank looked at Sam, embarrassed. "Please forgive my earlier rudeness. It's just that Norma always wanted the church to have a bigger kitchen and fellowship hall and I thought it would be wonderful if we could get it done while she was still around to see it happen. Didn't mean to be impolite."

"Don't think a thing of it," Sam said. "Let's keep a positive attitude and see what happens."

Hank reached across the table and shook Sam's hand. "Sounds like a plan."

Norma took Sam's hand. "We sure are happy to have you as our pastor."

"And I sure am happy to be your pastor," Sam said back, holding her hand and smiling.

It was days like this one that made Sam happy to be a pastor, sitting in a kitchen, working through the issues, providing comfort and hope, leaving each place a bit better than he had found it. The pay was rotten, but mornings like this caused him to remember that compensation came in many different forms, some of them too valuable to put a price tag on. He shook Hank's hand good-bye, hugged Norma, told them both he thought of them often and loved them, then went on his way, a wealthy man indeed.

26

It was a beautiful late fall day, not yet cold, a Windbreaker felt just right, and Sam enjoyed the walk home from the Witherses's house. He was getting to know his neighbors, the young couple with the newborn twins whose names he'd forgotten, the widower with the immaculate yard who always wanted to talk, the family with seven children whose house was a pleasant wreck. Barbara knew all their names, asked about them by name, after meeting them once. It would have been a great gift for a pastor to have, the easy recollection of names, and Sam envied her for it. She stood next to him at church gatherings and whispered the names of people in his ear as they approached.

He waved to the widower raking his yard, discussed the weather a moment, called out a hello to the young mother loading her twins in the car, and rounded the corner of the meetinghouse lane. There was an unfamiliar car in the meetinghouse parking lot. He hoped it wasn't a lawyer's. A man could take only so many lawyers in his life, after all. As he approached, the car door opened and a man stepped out, turning toward Sam.

The Quaker superintendent! It was too late to turn and run. He'd been seen. No hiding in the bushes.

Sam had known the superintendent nearly twenty years, had even liked him at one time, back when the superintendent had been a pastor, back before his promotion and his big head and pompous manner.

"Hello, Sam, my son." He was younger than Sam, but had the irritating habit of calling the pastors his sons and daughters, as if the Quakers had named him pope, which they most assuredly had not done.

"Well, look what the cat drug in," Sam said, his customary greeting upon seeing his superintendent, which thankfully wasn't often. "What brings you here?"

"It's been a while since I've seen you, and I wanted to come take you out for lunch," the superintendent said.

"Oh, what a shame. If you had called first, I could have told you I had lunch plans."

His plans were to eat a peanut-butter-and-jelly sandwich in his office while watching *The Andy Griffith Show* on YouTube, but his superintendent needn't know the details.

The superintendent frowned. "Can we talk just for a moment in your office?"

Sam realized there was no getting out of it.

"Sure, I have a few moments."

Sam sat at his desk, and invited the superintendent to take a seat on the couch.

"As you know," the superintendent began, "the quarterly committee meetings were held this past Saturday."

Sam hadn't known, since he made it a point to avoid as many meetings as he could.

"And the yearly meeting is dangerously low on funds," the superintendent continued.

"Perhaps we should lower administrative salaries," Sam suggested.

The superintendent made four times what Sam did and spent most of his time plotting for more pay and power.

"The finance committee has recommended that in addition to the yearly assessments each congregation pays, that each congregation now donate ten percent of its total income."

"Whose bright idea was this?" Sam asked.

"I suggested it, after considering a number of options."

"I don't see that flying," Sam said.

"Nevertheless, the finance committee has given their approval. The reason for my visit is that we've become aware of a rather large gift to your meeting. I wanted to give you ample notice so you can set aside the yearly meeting's share."

They hadn't even been given the money and already the buzzards were circling.

"I don't see that happening," Sam said. "This meeting hasn't seen hide nor hair of you for the past three years. They're not going to take kindly to you showing up asking for a hundred thousand dollars."

"I shouldn't have to remind you that the yearly meeting has authority over local congregations. If we want, we can close this church and seize all the assets. How many people are here? Twelve? Such a small congregation. Perhaps you should be consolidated with another meeting."

Adolf Hitler had had nothing on some church administrators.

"Being with you is always such a pleasure," Sam said, standing. "I always feel so deeply cared for after our little visits. But as much as I'd love to be with you, I have other things to do."

"Let's do this the easy way," the superintendent said, rising to his feet to leave. "It's only ten percent. That will leave you plenty of money. Perhaps I could even suggest to the elders that they give you a generous raise."

"If I need a raise, I can ask for myself," Sam said. "But I do appreciate your thoughtfulness."

He walked the superintendent to the door and thanked him for being a ray of sunshine in an otherwise dreary world. He returned to his desk, pulled his sandwich from the drawer, went on YouTube, and ate his lunch, watching *Andy Griffith* and wondering how one went about getting a superintendent fired. It would probably be easier to have him killed. The Mafia was onto something. Cement shoes, six miles off the coast, in the deep of night. He wondered how someone went about having that done. People like that didn't advertise in the yellow pages. Even if it cost the church fifty thousand dollars to have him knocked off, that would be a savings of fifty thousand, which was nothing to sneeze at. Probably no one would report the superintendent missing, either, not even his wife, who would figure it was best to quit while she was ahead.

It was a pleasant thought, but Sam had work to do, so he put aside those happy considerations, left the meetinghouse, and went forth to minister.

27

The funeral for Regina Charles was held the next day at 10 a.m. at the meetinghouse. Sam stood at the door, greeting people as they arrived. There were a surprising number of attenders, given Regina's personality. People she had grown up with, members of the congregation who had known Regina from her childhood, her lawyer Todd Cameron looking weasellike in his suit and gelled hair, and Gretchen Weber, the local veterinarian, kin to Ruby Hopper and Miriam Hodge, whom Sam had first met at Harmony Friends Meeting years before.

"A pleasure to see you, Gretchen," Sam said. "How did you know Regina?"

"When we were children, we went on several vacations together," Gretchen said. "My aunt Ruby, Olive Charles, Regina, and me." She leaned toward Sam and in a low voice said, "I never really liked her, but it's my day off and Aunt Ruby asked if I could come. I think she was afraid no one would be here."

"Well, we're glad you're here," Sam said.

He was especially glad, being somewhat infatuated with

Gretchen Weber. It was her French braid, Sam's great weakness. There was nothing so lovely on a woman as a French braid. A woman could weigh four hundred pounds and have a goiter the size of a football on her neck, but if she had a French braid, Sam would fall in love with her. For thirty years he'd tried to talk Barbara into growing her hair long enough for a French braid, but she'd refused, not wanting the fuss and bother.

"I hope you've been well," Sam added.

"Very well, thank you. And how are you and Barbara and the boys?"

"Fine, thanks for asking. Barbara's working at the elementary school as the librarian. Levi is still up at Purdue and Addison is enjoying military life."

"And how about you, Sam?" Gretchen asked. "How do you like it here?"

"So far, so good. Nice folks, the meeting is growing. People are getting along pretty well."

The last sentence wasn't entirely true, but maybe if Sam said it enough times, it would happen.

"Aunt Ruby told me about the money Olive left the meeting. What are you all going to do with a million dollars?"

"I don't have the slightest idea," Sam said.

"Oh, I'm sure some people in the meeting will be making some very specific suggestions," Gretchen said, laughing.

She had a lovely laugh. Her eyes got caught up in it. Blue eyes, the color of a bright summer sky. Warm and vivid.

"We'd love to have you join us if you ever have a free Sunday," Sam said.

"I've been thinking of attending," Gretchen said. "I brought another veterinarian into the practice last week, so won't be working weekends much longer."

For a moment Sam imagined the joy of looking out into the congregation and seeing Gretchen Weber with her French braid and blue eyes, then remembered he was married and felt bad, then felt even worse for not feeling as guilty as he should have felt.

Leonard and Wanda Fink approached the meetinghouse, which snapped Sam out of his reverie. He welcomed them inside. The Finks, he was learning, were the kind of church members who attended every event held at the meetinghouse, invited or not. Weddings, funerals, Bible studies. Leonard attended women's meetings. Wanda attended men's meetings. When a singles' group had met at the meetinghouse several years before, Wanda and Leonard had attended that, too. And they didn't just sit there quietly, either. They whined and wheedled their way into leadership, controlling, dominating, eventually taking over, like cancer. Two pastors ago, Wanda had been in charge of the men's Bible study. Go figure.

"How did you know Regina?" he asked the Finks as they entered.

"We didn't," Wanda said.

"Well, I'm sure she would have been happy to see you here," Sam said.

"Happy at her funeral, I don't think so," Leonard said. Leonard Fink had lately been getting more snippy with Sam.

"So where do you stand on this church addition?" Wanda asked. "It's a waste of money, as far as I'm concerned."

"Let's not talk about that just now," Sam said. "It's time for the funeral to start."

Sam made his way to the front of the meetingroom, to the facing bench, and took a seat beside Ruby Hopper, who had agreed to deliver the eulogy. That had taken a load off, since he'd been in no mood to say nice things about someone who'd hired a lawyer to sue him. He opened the memorial service by thanking everyone for attending, then launched into a prayer thanking God for Regina and her aunt Olive and for all the saints of the church who had taught them so much. He asked God to make them more saintlike, to make them more like Regina, who had had many wonderful qualities, none of which came to mind immediately, so he didn't elaborate. Deep into the prayer, he remembered that Ruby had asked him to invite people to stay for a funeral dinner immediately following the service, so he thanked God for the food they would soon enjoy and invited everyone to stay, then sputtered to a stop with a weak *amen*, having grown exhausted trying to pray himself out of a corner.

They entered into Quaker silence, then Ruby stood to speak, talking for a brief time about Regina, straining to say something nice, the littlest thing, then finally mentioned Regina had always enjoyed eating pies, blueberry pies to be precise, and then Ruby paused, as if Regina's appetite merited deeper, more prayerful consideration.

"And her aunt Olive loved her very much, despite the poor choices she made," Ruby declared, by way of closing. "She told me so many times."

With that reminder of love, that even people like Regina had someone who cared about them, they concluded the service. There was no body to haul to a graveyard for a burial, Regina having opted for cremation, so the men set up tables, while the women gathered in the kitchen to serve the food. Fried chicken, mashed potatoes with white gravy, green beans, carrots, and three kinds of pies, made from scratch by Ruby Hopper, since Olive Charles would have wanted it that way, it being her niece's funeral dinner and not a time to skimp.

Sam carried the urn containing Regina's ashes to his office, then helped serve the meal. When everyone had been served, he sat down next to Ruby Hopper, who was seated across from Gretchen Weber, who looked lovely even while eating fried chicken. It took a beautiful woman to look good while gnawing on a chicken leg, but Gretchen Weber pulled it off.

Not for the first time, Sam wondered if he was fit to be a pastor. True ministers didn't have those kinds of feelings, did they? One of his professors in seminary had talked about it once during class, advising them to pray for God's help when tempted. Sam had done just that the three times he'd seen Gretchen Weber, but God hadn't seemed in a hurry to help Sam. He still had those feelings. He loved his wife, that wasn't the problem. It was Gretchen Weber, she was a siren luring a sailor toward the rocks. He wondered if maybe he needed some Mormon underwear to resist temptation, fend off evil influences, and stand firmly for the right.

He excused himself and finished his dinner in the kitchen, visiting with Wilson Roberts, who talked at length about toilets and other plumbing fixtures, driving every thought of romance from Sam's mind.

28

How did Regina's funeral go?" Barbara asked that night at the supper table.

"Had 'em weeping," Sam said, his customary response whenever Barbara asked about a funeral service. "Actually, it went very well. Ruby gave a nice eulogy, there was a good crowd, the food was delicious. It was a nice send-off for someone who was suing us."

"Who all was there?"

"Oh, let me see, Ruby, the Finks, Wilson Roberts, Regina's lawyer, Olive's lawyer, some people I didn't know. They told me their names, but I've forgotten them. That's about it."

"I thought I saw Gretchen Weber walking out with Ruby," Barbara said.

"Oh yeah. I forgot about her. I guess she was there. Say, this soup is really delicious, honey. I think I'll have another bowl."

Barbara laughed. "You are so transparent. Like you actually forgot your fantasy girl was there."

It was scary how well she knew him.

"She is not my fantasy girl," he said.

"Little Miss Veterinarian with her French braid," Barbara said. "Is that why you've always wanted me to have a French braid?"

"I like you just the way you are," he said.

Barbara was perilously close to the truth. He was starting to squirm. What was it with women, anyway? It was as if men walked around with their every thought written in a bubble over their heads, like Snoopy in the comics.

"Do you know you talk in your sleep?" Barbara asked.

"What's that got to do with anything?"

"Oh, nothing. Except the first night we moved in here, when Gretchen came over with Ruby to welcome us, you said her name in your sleep."

"I did not," Sam said.

"You most certainly did. Several times, in fact. And your tongue was hanging out. You were panting like a dog."

"Then why is this the first time I've heard of this?" Sam asked.

"Oh, because I wasn't too worried about it. I trust you. I can trust you, can't I? You wouldn't leave me for Gretchen Weber, would you?"

"Of course not. Don't even say that."

"Just checking," Barbara said. "A woman likes to know where she stands with her man."

They did the dishes standing side by side, Barbara washing, Sam drying and putting away. They talked about the boys and the million dollars the church would soon inherit and his parents moving in down the street and the possibility of Sam's brother, Roger, marrying Christina Pringle, and Otis Pringle being in their family, perhaps coming to their house for Thanksgiving and Christmas and ruining their lives. After they'd cleaned up, Sam sat at the kitchen table and went online on Barbara's laptop and Googled "Mormon underwear," which directed him to www.mormonskivvies.com, where he ordered a set of temple undergarments. They looked warm and winter was fast approaching. Besides, he'd always tried to be open to different religious expressions. Maybe the Mormons were onto something. It wouldn't hurt to try. Perhaps they would help him forget all about Gretchen Weber.

"What are you doing?" Barbara asked, watching him type in their credit card number.

"Ordering some long underwear for winter," he answered.

"Are they the red kind with the flap on the butt?"

"You mean a union suit? Not hardly."

"I always kind of liked those," Barbara said. "My grandpa used to wear them."

"So did mine," Sam said. "But my grandmother wore a mink stole in the winter. I'd go to hug her and there'd be a dead little mink face staring me in the eye, snarling at me."

"I remember those."

This was what Sam enjoyed most about Barbara, their discussions of obscure topics. He could probably never talk about dead minks with Gretchen, she being a veterinarian and likely opposed to the wearing of fur.

"My grandmother also wore a girdle and these thingumajigs that held up her hosiery," Sam recalled. "Not that I ever saw them on her. But she draped them over the radiator to dry. They were elastic straps with rubber snaps that attached to the stockings. What were those called?"

"Garter belts and suspenders," Barbara said.

"Didn't you wear those on our wedding night?" Sam asked.

"Brides typically do, and yes, I did."

With that, Sam promptly forgot all about Gretchen Weber and began whispering vague French-like words in Barbara's ear, which culminated in a most pleasant interaction.

Afterward they lay side by side, discussing their plans for Christmas. It was his parents' turn to have them.

"It'll be nice to have Addison home," Sam said. "I'm going to ask the elders if I can have the following Sunday off, so I won't have to write a sermon the week he's home."

"This will be the last Christmas in your parents' house. It feels kind of weird."

"Yeah, I'm going to miss that old house," Sam said. "I can't believe they're moving. I thought we were going to carry them out of that house."

"Are they even going to be able to have visitors? They're moving right after the New Year. I imagine their house is all torn up. Wouldn't you think?"

"I would think so, but you know Mom and Dad. If we don't go, we'll never hear the end of it," Sam said. "Besides, they're probably counting on us helping them move."

That gave them pause. They lay in bed, contemplating a week off from work packing boxes, loading furniture in a truck, throwing stuff away when his parents weren't watching.

"Aren't they going to hire movers?" Barbara asked.

"You know my dad. He's going to say, 'Why do I need to hire someone to move me? I've got two able-bodied sons and two grandsons.' There's no way he's going to hire a mover. We'll be lucky if he rents a U-Haul truck."

"I do not want to spend the entire time Addison is home on leave helping your parents move."

Sam didn't respond. He knew how the week of Christmas would play out. Them working like borrowed mules to get his folks packed up, out of the house, and up to Hope. No sense fighting it. The worst part would be his dad's nostalgia. He would throw nothing away. There would be no lightening of the load. When Sam was a kid, during a terrific summer storm, lightning had struck a tree in their yard, splitting it down the middle. When they'd cut the tree into firewood, his father had kept the lightning-struck section of the trunk, intending to make a coffee table. That had been forty years ago, and the hunk of wood was still in their garage. His father would insist on bringing it with them. That was just the start of it. There were his license plate collection, his antique wrench collection, old mattresses, snow tires from cars sold long ago, half-empty paint cans, the paint solidified, power tools with electrical shorts that electrocuted the user. All of it would be hauled a hundred miles north for Sam to deal with after his parents died. It exhausted him to think of it. He fell to sleep praying a wandering arsonist would stop by his parents' house while they were out to supper at the Long John Silver's in Cartersburg and torch the place.

"Yes, Lord," he prayed. "Just one arsonist. That's all I need. Just one."

29

~

Sam was out the door right behind Barbara the next morning and over to the office to work on his sermon before the phone started ringing. Two hours into the morning, he heard a hammering sound and looked out the window to see Hank Withers and Wayne Newby, the latter balancing on crutches, driving wooden stakes into the meetinghouse lawn. What was this about?

He pulled on his jacket and went outside.

"Hey, guys," he said. "What's up?"

"Mornin', Sam," Hank said. "Just wanted to get a better idea of how big the addition was going to be, so we're staking it out."

His gut tightened as he imagined Wanda Fink's reaction when she drove up to the meetinghouse and saw survey stakes pounded into the lawn.

Hank paced off thirty steps, counting aloud.

"Now the kitchen will be in that corner over there," he said, gesturing across the space. He paused, studying the meetinghouse. "But you know, the more I think about it, maybe what we ought to do is turn our old worship space into a fellow-ship hall, since we already have plumbing there, and build a new worship room. That'll save us the cost of plumbing the new addition. Then we just expand and update our existing kitchen. What do you think, Sam?"

Sam thought Wanda Fink was going to scratch out their eyes when she got wind of this.

"That's a fine idea," Wayne Newby said. "That'll give us more worship space. There were twenty-four of us at worship last Sunday. That's up from twelve when Sam first started. At this rate we're going to need more room for worship."

Sam felt a delicious tickle of pride. He ran the figures in his head. From twelve to twenty-four, doubling the church in five months. Not bad. Not bad at all. It was mostly due to the Woodrums, who knew a zillion people and felt free to invite them to meeting for worship, something the average Quaker would no more do than walk naked down Main Street, which was why the average Quaker meeting was dying on the vine, though Sam didn't point that out.

"Did you get permission to drive these stakes in?" Sam asked. "It might upset some folks, since we've not yet made the decision to build."

"Just doing what you told me to do, Sam," Hank said. "Re-member? You suggested that me and Wilson and Wayne and Dan make a presentation about the project so people could see what we were talking about. I thought it would help if folks could actually see the size of the space we're talking about."

"I would prefer you not tell others I asked you to do this," Sam said. "I don't need the trouble."

This was the way it usually worked in the church—someone did something that made someone else mad and the pastor got blamed. Over the course of his ministerial career Sam had been blamed for the elections of Bill Clinton and Barack Obama, the price of gasoline, the spread of communism, the destruction of the World Trade Center, and the increase of teen pregnancy, though he had never personally impregnated any teen, nor did he have any intention of doing so.

"Keep me out of it," Sam said. "I just work here."

"Fair enough, just come hold the end of this tape measure and then you can get right back to your office work," Hank said.

"No thank you," Sam said. "If I hold the end of the tape measure, Wanda Fink will ask who did this, and you will say, 'Me and Wayne and Sam,' and I'll never hear the end of it."

"Let me hold it," Wayne Newby said, hobbling over. "I'm not afraid of Wanda Fink."

"That's because Wanda Fink can't get you fired," Sam pointed out. "She can only annoy you. Making her mad won't jeopardize your livelihood, cause you to lose your living quarters, deplete your savings, and plunge you into bankruptcy."

So there.

It occurred to Sam this might be a good time to talk with Wayne about his fascination with *Playboy*, so he asked Wayne to stop in his office before he left, which Wayne did, fifteen minutes later, after he and Hank had strung yellow tape around the stakes.

"What's on your mind?" Wayne said, easing himself down into a chair.

"Glad to see you up and around so soon."

"I was going stir-crazy. I had to get out of the house. Doreen was driving me nuts."

"How is Doreen?"

"Fine. Tired. She's been mad at me ever since she found that old *Playboy*."

"Did she find the others?" Sam asked.

"What do you mean, others?"

"The ones the mailman has been bringing. The ones you tip him five dollars to deliver when Doreen isn't home."

"How'd you know about that?" Wayne demanded.

"The mailman told me."

"Why'd he do that? What business is it of his?"

"Probably none of his business," Sam said. "But that's beside the point. The point is, if he told me, he's probably told others, and Doreen is bound to find out sooner or later. You might consider switching to *National Geographic*."

"Won't work," Wayne said. "She said it's just as bad as *Playboy*, that African boobs are the same as American boobs. She says boobs are boobs."

"Maybe you should confine your sexual interest to your wife," Sam suggested. "It isn't good for your marriage to focus on other women."

Wayne stared straight ahead, frowning, coming to grips with a life without *Playboy*.

"Yeah, you're probably right," he said after a while. "I'm too old for that nonsense anyway. I'm going to throw them away."

"Intimacy isn't nonsense," Sam said. "Just work to keep it within your marriage. Doreen deserves that, and so do you."

"I was getting tired of hiding them anyway. It's a lot of work to keep something hidden."

"Yes, it sure is," Sam said, thinking how quickly Barbara had sniffed out Gretchen Weber.

"Thanks for not saying anything in front of Hank."

"Well, it's none of his business," Sam said. "It might not even be any of my business. I just want you and Doreen to have a happy marriage."

"I appreciate it, Sam."

They chatted a bit longer, mostly about growing older and the changes it required, then Wayne took his leave.

It had been a good conversation, perhaps even transformative, and Sam sat at his desk wishing he could use it for a sermon illustration. He probably couldn't, though. A minister could change the setting and the sinner's gender, but people still figured out who you were talking about. He remembered, years before, speaking against alcohol and telling a story about a woman losing her child because of drunkenness. His father had piped up after the sermon, in the silence, and said, "I think you're talking about Ralph Hodge, aren't you?" No, maybe he would avoid the topic of pornography for the foreseeable future. Besides, it was enough to know Wayne was headed in a better direction. That was reward enough.

30

The FedEx man delivered Sam's Mormon skivvies three days later, which was coincidentally the date of the first cold snap of the year, so Sam wasted no time putting them on. They were tight and uncomfortable and immediately took his mind off of Gretchen Weber, so Sam was pleased with the purchase. At noon he bundled up and walked to Bruno's and ordered lasagna. It was well past one thirty and the restaurant was empty, so Bruno sat and discussed pasta with Sam.

"There are six hundred kinds of pasta," Bruno said, shaking his head at the wonder of it. "Six hundred! Of course, I don't sell all six hundred. I have about a dozen. I sell mostly spaghetti, but people buy a lot of lasagna, too. Manicotti is pretty popular, too."

"Barbara likes manicotti," Sam said. "It's her favorite."

At the mention of Barbara's name, Bruno smiled. "Oh, your wife, she's a lovely woman. If anything ever happens to you, I want to marry her."

"Well, I'm in excellent health, so don't get your hopes up."

It had been no secret to Sam that Bruno wanted him dead so he could comfort Sam's grieving widow and move in on her.

The bell over the door jingled and Sam glanced over to see who had entered. He was grateful to have a witness so Bruno wouldn't stab him in the chest and claim Sam had fallen on a knife.

It was Gretchen Weber. And even though he was wearing his Mormon skivvies, which were supposed to help him resist temptation, fend off evil influences, and stand firmly for the right, he felt a stirring and thought to himself that if Barbara died, he would marry Gretchen Weber. He was ashamed the moment he thought it. If Barbara kicked the bucket that day, he would never forgive himself.

Gretchen walked across the restaurant toward them. Bruno stood. Sam said hello, trying to appear casual.

"Hi, Sam," she said. "Do you mind if I sit with you?"

No, he didn't mind, not at all, though he should have. He should have minded a great deal, given his feelings for her. Instead he stood up and invited Gretchen to join him.

He was almost finished with his lasagna, but wanted to stretch out his meal, so asked Bruno to bring him strawberry cheesecake, which he nibbled on while Gretchen ate. He was nervous, but also enchanted, and couldn't bring himself to leave, not with Gretchen across the table looking beautiful with her French braid.

"How do you do that hair thingy?" he asked, then silently cursed himself. Hair thingy? She'd think he was an idiot.

"Oh, you mean my French braid. It's easy. Maybe one day I'll show you how."

Was she flirting? Sam thought maybe she was. What had he

done? He had turned a perfectly innocent veterinarian into a vixen.

"I think maybe I better go," he said. "I have quite a bit of work to get done."

He said good-bye to Gretchen, paid Bruno, and left, ashamed of himself and angry with the manufacturers of Mormon temple garments, who had obviously made a shoddy product that was utterly useless in warding off temptation.

A new coffee shop had opened up down the street from the meetinghouse, so he stopped and bought Barbara a nonfat caffè latte, a guilt offering, then went past the school to give it to her. He signed in at the office, then walked the hallway down to the library, where he found her standing amid a clutch of small children. She didn't notice him at first, so he watched her a short while. She was a beautiful woman. He could see why Bruno wanted him dead.

She turned, saw him, and smiled. "Look who's here. Children, this is my husband, Mr. Gardner."

"Hello, Mr. Gardner," the children chorused.

"Hi, kids. I brought your librarian a nonfat caffè latte." He handed Barbara her drink.

She smiled, then leaned forward to hug him. "I expect you'll tell me tonight what you did to feel guilty enough to bring me a latte," she whispered in his ear.

The woman was a bloodhound. She could smell shame and fear a mile away.

"Can't a man just bring his wife a little treat because he loves her?" Sam asked.

"Of course he can. I was just teasing you," she said. "You're sweet to do this."

Whew!

He stayed a bit longer and read to the children, hamming it up, doing all he could to get on his wife's good side so that if someone said to her, "Oh, by the way, I saw your husband having lunch with Gretchen Weber at Bruno's," she wouldn't believe them.

As he was walking home, his phone buzzed in his pocket. Doreen Newby's name flashed on the screen. Sam debated whether to answer. He was learning there was no such thing as a brief phone conversation with Doreen Newby. But if he didn't talk with her now, she'd keep calling until he answered.

"Hi, Doreen. How are you?"

"Terrible. Are you at the meetinghouse?"

"Not now, but I will be in about five minutes. Did you need something?"

"I need to talk with you. Wayne's done it again."

"What has Wayne done again?" Sam asked. "Can you be more specific?"

"Gone and cheated on me, that's what."

Not for the first time in his ministry, Sam wished some people would keep their marital problems to themselves.

"Do you want to meet and talk?" he asked, hoping against hope she would say no.

"I'm in the meetinghouse parking lot right now, waiting for you. Can you hurry it up?"

"I'll be right there," Sam said, speeding his pace.

He was sweating inside his Mormon temple garments. He wondered how in the world Mormons wore these things in the summer. It was like standing in front of a blast furnace. Maybe they were too weary from heat to sin. Maybe that's how the skivvies thing was supposed to work. By the time he reached the meetinghouse lane, sweat was pouring from him.

Doreen Newby was stalking back and forth in front of the meetinghouse door, on the verge of eruption.

She turned and saw him. "He's gone and done it now. I'm leaving him for good this time."

Doreen had seemed so nice when he had first met her, so solicitous and kind. When he had first visited the Newbys' home, they had seemed happy together, so well suited to each other. Now this.

"Doreen, what in the world is going on?" Sam asked as he ushered her into his office. "Take a seat and let's talk."

And that was when the ugly truth came out.

31

Wayne was gone," Doreen said, wiping the back of her hand across her runny nose. "I don't ordinarily go on his computer. I can't do it very well. But I wanted to look up a telephone number. I wish we still had phone books. I never can find a number when I need it."

She went on for a few minutes, railing against progress and change, ruing the day computers had been invented. Sam steered her back to the topic.

"So you were on the computer, and what happened?"

"I saw Wayne's e-mail, and there was a letter on it that proves he's been cheating on me."

This wasn't the first time Sam had heard of illicit affairs conducted over the Internet. *What is it with people anyway?* he wondered. People having affairs used to sneak off to fleabag hotels and keep to themselves. Now they tracked down old flames on Facebook and were too dumb to hide the evidence. Then their spouses found out and had to face the realization that their husband or wife wasn't just unfaithful, but stupid.

"It was an e-mail from a man," Doreen sniffed.

"Are you saying Wayne is gay? I never would have guessed that," Sam said. "Of course, some people become very good at hiding their sexual orientation. I'm sure when Wayne first realized he was gay, he didn't feel he could be honest about it. People weren't as accepting then as they are now."

"Don't be stupid. He isn't gay. It was an e-mail from a man wanting to buy his *Playboy* collection. Collection! I didn't even know he had a collection. I thought he just had the one I found in the garage. I tore the house apart looking for it, but can't find it. I tried calling him, but he won't pick up his phone. He's all the time letting the battery run down. At least that's the excuse he gives."

Sam's mind was racing. Wayne was selling his magazine collection? What an idiot! He had promised Sam he would throw it away.

Sam's phone buzzed in his pocket. He eased it out and studied the screen discreetly. Wayne Newby. Speak of the devil.

"Doreen, I'm sorry, but I need to answer this. Do you mind?"

She frowned, but nodded permission.

Sam answered his phone.

"Sam, is that you? This is Wayne. Is Doreen there? I think she's been on my computer and found out about our collection."

Our collection? What in the world did he mean by that?

"If she's there, just say yes," Wayne said.

"Yes."

"I know I was supposed to throw them away," Wayne went on. "But I went online and there's people who pay good money for them. So I put the whole collection on eBay. You should see the e-mails I've been getting. One fella offered me a thousand dollars for the whole shebang. Of course I wasn't going to keep it. I was going to give the money to the church towards a new roof. So it's kinda our collection now."

Sam was relatively confident theirs would be the first church maintenance project funded by the sale of pornography.

"What you do with the money is up to you," Sam said. "It's your collection, not ours."

Doreen eyed him. "Is that Wayne? If that's him, you tell him to get over here right now."

"Wayne, Doreen wants you to come over to the meeting-house," Sam said.

Wayne groaned.

"Might as well face her now and get it over with," Sam said.

Wayne was there ten minutes later.

"So, Mr. Smut, a man e-mailed you wanting to buy your collection of *Playboy* magazines," Doreen said the moment Wayne walked in the office. "What collection would that be? Because I don't know of any collection. I suppose the man had you confused for someone else."

"I collected them for the articles," Wayne said. "I never looked at the pictures, I swear."

"How long have you been reading the articles and where are they now?" Doreen asked.

Wayne thought for a moment, counting on his fingers. "Twenty-two years, and I rented a storage unit at that place across from the Moose Lodge on Highway 40. I kept 'em there."

"You told me you rented that to store your parents' furniture, that you couldn't bear to throw it away."

"It's all there, the furniture and the, uh, literature," Wayne said.

"Literature, my foot. Wayne Newby, you are going to be the death of me."

Sam thought he might put in a good word for Wayne. Despite his efforts to cheat their insurance company he was a decent trustee and Sam wanted to stay on his good side. "To be fair, Doreen, Wayne and I had talked about this matter several days ago and he had decided to get rid of them."

"That's right," Wayne said. "I was getting rid of them. I want nothing more to do with them. And to make up for it, I'm going to give all the money I make selling them to the church."

"You promise to get rid of them and never look at one again?" Doreen said.

"I give my word," Wayne said, raising his right hand as if swearing an oath.

"Doreen, can you forgive Wayne and move forward with your marriage?" Sam asked.

"I suppose we've been married too long to give up now," she said.

"Wayne, can you pay more attention to Doreen and not spend so much time in the basement with your model trains and stop reading *Playboy* and take her places every now and then?" Sam said.

"Yeah, I've been kind of lonely lately," Wayne admitted.

Doreen began to weep, sitting in Sam's office. A trickle at first, then a sob and a heave, then she went and sat on Wayne's lap, which was excruciating for Wayne, whose recently broken leg was still tender. But he said nothing, bravely bearing the pain as a penance for being stupid.

32

A memory.

Sam was eight years old when Art Drucker, who owned Art's One-Hour Cleaners in Harmony, put a sign on his front door announcing the dry cleaner's was closed and would be for the foreseeable future. He gave the store key to Bob Miles, publisher of the *Harmony Herald*, whose office was next door, and wrote on the sign that anyone with clothes at the cleaners could get the key from Bob and retrieve their clothing, which everyone did, including a few men who'd never been customers of Art's but were in the market for a slightly used suit, freshly cleaned.

Sam's father lost his suit, but three weeks later noticed Owen Stout, the lawyer, wearing one just like it.

"Owen Stout wouldn't steal," Sam's mother said.

"There's no telling what people will do if given the chance," Sam's father said.

Owen Stout, a lawyer, an officer of the court, a seeker of justice, a stealer of suits.

A few nights later, they had been eating supper when Charlie Gardner said to no one in particular, "Well, I learned today where Art Drucker went."

"I heard Doris's father died and they went down to Florida for the funeral," Sam's mother said.

"If that's where he went, he forgot to take Doris. I saw her today at the hardware store buying new door locks," Charlie Gardner said.

"Why would she need new door locks?" Sam asked. "What's wrong with her old ones?"

"Her husband has a key to the old locks, that's why."

Gloria Gardner frowned. "Charles, let's not talk about this in front of the children."

"Talk about what?" Sam asked, his curiosity heightened. "What don't you want Dad to talk about?"

"She doesn't want me to talk about Art Drucker running off with Nate Griffith's wife," Charlie Gardner said. "Even though he did and everyone in town knows it."

"I never did trust that man," Gloria Gardner said. "He was always leering at me."

"What's leering?" Sam asked.

"Never mind. Charles, why did you have to mention this at the dinner table?"

That night Sam's father came into the bedroom Sam shared with his brother and gave his sons the TALK. He discussed at length the mating rituals of geese, swans, and various members of the avian family, then said they would one day meet a young lady and fall in love and get married and that when they did they shouldn't run off to Cincinnati with their neighbor's wife.

"Is that where Art Drucker went, to Cincinnati?" Sam asked.

"Yep. Lives three blocks from Riverfront Stadium and has season tickets to the Reds," Charlie Gardner said.

"Wow! That's great," Sam's brother, Roger, said. "I wish I lived three blocks from Riverfront Stadium. I can see why he left."

"Don't tell your mother that," their father warned.

"Maybe we could go visit him," Sam said. "Maybe on a day when the Reds are playing the Dodgers."

Adultery was starting to sound enticing, which wasn't the direction in which Charlie Gardner had wanted their conversation to head.

"There's things more important than baseball," he said. "Sure, Art Drucker can see the Reds play, but he's broken his wife's heart and hurt his children. I bet if he had to do it over again, he'd choose differently."

"Yeah, maybe he'd have moved to Chicago instead," Roger said. "Then he could see the White Sox and the Cubs."

The next day Sam saw Doris Drucker at Kivett's Five and Dime. His mother was shopping for new pants, and Sam was leaning against the magazine rack reading the comic books when Doris walked past, her head down, lost in thought. She looked worn and haggard, so burdened even a ten-year-old could sense something was amiss.

"Hi, Mrs. Drucker. I heard about Mr. Drucker running off with Nate Griffith's wife. I sure am sorry."

"Where did you hear that?"

"My dad told me. He said everyone in town knew."

Doris Drucker and her three children left town the next week and Sam never saw them again, though he thought of them every time he walked past where the dry cleaner's had been. After a few months it became a bakery, which lasted less than a year, then Owen Stout bought it for his law office and had been there ever since. The building a reminder of stolen suits and stolen love.

Two years later Art Drucker and Nate Griffith's wife moved back to town. She returned to Nate, and the minister from the Baptist church came to see them and they went to counseling and got themselves saved and were still together, out in the country, west of town. Art Drucker rented the apartment over Owen Stout's law office, got cancer five years later, and died. His funeral was held at Mackey's Funeral Home. Johnny Mackey was there, along with Pastor Taylor, and Art's brother from Terre Haute, and a nephew, but no one else. The town had sided with Doris and the children. If you ran off to Cincinnati with another man's wife, then came back, it was difficult to make your way back into polite society. Art died alone and bitter. They didn't find his body for four days, when Owen noticed a smell, got his key, unlocked the door, went upstairs, and found Art in the bathroom, where he'd slipped and busted his head open on the bathtub. The cancer had been in his prostate. He'd had another ten years in him, maybe more, if the bathtub hadn't gotten him.

"I hope he learned his lesson," Charlie Gardner said.

The general opinion in town was that Art Drucker hadn't learned his lesson at all, and had died unrepentant and was now in hell, where he would spend all eternity being poked with pitchforks by Satan and his imps. The Baptist minister had visited Art and had given him every opportunity to get right with the Lord but Art had refused.

"Pride goeth before a fall," Sam's mother had told him. "Art Drucker was too proud. He hadn't always been that way. Back before he owned the dry cleaner's he was a regular man. Then he hit it big in business and it went to his head."

That a dry cleaning shop was considered big business was an indication of how little it took to succeed in Harmony.

These many years later, whenever Sam thought of Gretchen Weber, his mind turned immediately to Art Drucker living above Owen Stout's law office, and of the lonely death that awaited those who spurned the Lord.

33

Addison arrived home on leave two days before Christmas. Sam and Barbara met him at the airport, delirious with joy. He had lost twenty pounds and grown two inches, and was ramrod-straight. He called Sam "sir" and Barbara "ma'am," and when they stopped for lunch, he removed his hat when they entered the restaurant and thanked the hostess who seated them. The army, it appeared, had accomplished in six months what Sam and Barbara had labored eighteen years to achieve—the creation of a well-mannered young man. When the check arrived, he picked it up before Sam could snag it.

"My treat," he told Sam. "I'm working now."

Sam didn't know whether to be proud or depressed. He had always enjoyed treating his sons and felt as if the baton had been passed and he was no longer needed. On the other hand, he had just saved thirty-nine dollars.

Levi arrived home from Purdue that evening with Monica, whose minister mother was deep in the throes of Christmas at her Methodist church and unable to fetch Monica home.

Quakers were comparatively relaxed when it came to religious holidays, which Sam appreciated. Harmony Friends Meeting had sponsored a progressive nativity scene until it had gotten too big and had to be turned over to the town, which had pleased Sam to no end. "Let the town have it," he'd said. He was glad to be shed of it. Sure, someone would sue the town and the Supreme Court would eventually say the town couldn't sponsor a progressive nativity scene, but that would take years to happen and Sam would be dead or gone by then. Sure enough, he was gone now. From what he could tell of Hope Meeting, it didn't go overboard at Christmas. Some extra hymns, hats and mittens for orphans, and pies for the folks at the county home. Maybe a few songs for them, too.

Barbara fixed chili and they stayed up late playing board games and reminiscing. The boys made fun of one another, which was their custom, while Sam grilled Monica about the Methodist retirement plan for its ministers. It turned out to be vastly superior to the Quaker retirement plan for its ministers, which centered around the theme of "trust in the Lord," meaning the pastors shouldn't depend upon the Quakers for retirement assistance of any sort. But the night was so perfect, with both his sons at home, that even the prospect of a retirement spent in poverty couldn't faze Sam.

As for Barbara, it warmed her heart to see her family together, enjoying one another. For the past several days, she had worried it was falling apart. A teacher at her school had made a catty remark about seeing Sam at Bruno's with another woman.

"Probably one of the church ladies," Barbara had said.

"Didn't look like any church lady I've ever seen."

Barbara hadn't asked Sam about it, though she had been

thinking about it ever since. It wasn't that she didn't trust him. She did. But he could be so clueless. It would be just like Sam to be seduced and not even be aware of it. She'd have to keep an eye on things, make sure he didn't get himself into trouble.

The next day was Christmas Eve. They slept in, enjoyed a late breakfast, packed their suitcases, deposited Monica at her home, and drove to Harmony to be with Sam's parents. They looped through the town, driving past their old home, slowing to look at it. There was no one home, but the house was unlocked, so Sam and the boys poked their heads in and looked around. The Grants had painted the interior, except for the strip behind the dining room curtains where the boy's heights had been recorded over the years. The boys stood with their backs against the wall once more while Sam marked and dated their heights.

"Would you look at that," Sam marveled. "Who would have ever thought you'd grow that tall."

They nosed around a bit longer, then went back outside to where Barbara was seated in the car, waiting.

"Were the Grants home?" she asked.

"No," Sam answered.

"What took you so long, then?"

"We went inside to see what they had done with the place."

"Dad marked our heights on the dining room wall," Addison said.

"You know, I might be wrong, but it's not our house any longer, so maybe you shouldn't just go in there like you own the place," Barbara said.

"Uly wouldn't mind. He said when he bought it that we were welcome anytime."

"I imagine he meant you were welcome to visit anytime when they were home. He probably didn't mean you should just walk into their house whenever you wanted and write on their walls."

Sam considered that for a moment. "Yeah, you might be right."

"So what did it look like?" Barbara asked.

"They painted the whole inside."

"What color?"

"Kind of a yellowy cream color, I suppose."

"Except your old bedroom," Levi said. "It's green."

"Uly keeps his underwear in the bottom drawer of their dresser," Sam remarked. "You'd think he would get sore bending down like that all the time."

"You went through their dresser drawers?" Barbara asked, incredulous.

"I wanted to see if the drawers were dovetailed," Sam explained. "They were. Beautiful dresser. Cherrywood. Antique."

Barbara shook her head, amazed. "You had no right to do that."

Sam began laughing. "Fooled you. Geez, what kind of a clod do you think I am?"

In the backseat, Addison and Levi snotted themselves laughing.

Barbara suspected it was going to be a long Christmas holiday.

They pulled into the Gardner driveway, and Sam's mother hurried to greet them, weeping when she saw Addison. "I never thought I'd see you again," she wailed. "I was afraid you'd be killed."

"Grandma, I never left the country."

"I know, but with these crazy Taliban you never know. Not to mention Saddam Hussein."

"Uh, Mom, Saddam Hussein is dead," Sam pointed out.

"Well, thank God for that. That man was up to no good. Oh, look how tall you've gotten," she said, standing at arm's length from Addison, admiring him. "And so strong. What happened to the little boy who used to sit on my lap?"

She fussed over Addison a bit longer, then made a fuss over Levi so he wouldn't feel left out, then led them indoors and began feeding them. Sam's father was in the basement, packing up boxes to move north. He'd been at it for a month and had only packed two boxes, studying each item, determining whether he might need it in the future. So far he had pitched out a broken pair of pliers and a box of used furnace filters.

"I don't know how in the world he expects to be done by the New Year," Gloria Gardner said. "Sam, could you and the boys help us pack?"

"Mom, I think the only way this is going to work is if you and Dad go somewhere for a few days and let us do what needs to be done. Otherwise Dad will want to keep everything and we'll be here forever."

But Charlie Gardner had not been an avid collector of all things useless for sixty years only to entrust his valuables to someone else in a moment of duress. "Absolutely not," he told his wife later that night. "Sam has no idea what these things are worth. You think I can just turn everything over to him? He wouldn't have the faintest clue what to do with some of these things."

They woke up early on Christmas Day, ate a hefty breakfast that left them dopey, then opened their presents, which were modest this year, the adults not needing anything and the boys too old to want much. A package of underwear and an iTunes gift card for each of the boys, a pocketknife for Sam, and three books for Barbara. Sam gave his parents a box of sixty-gallon construction-grade trash bags, hoping they'd get the hint. They spent the rest of the day packing, with Gloria distracting Charles while Sam and the boys crammed junk in the trash bags and hauled them out to the curb. After three days they were done with half the basement, and had two and a half floors to go, along with the garage and mini-barn, which put them on track to have Charles and Gloria Gardner packed and moved three months after they had promised to turn the house over to Deena, who stopped past each afternoon to measure their progress and worry.

34

W hat I'd like to do," Charles Gardner told Sam on the last day of their visit, "is buy the house that woman left to your meeting."

"Olive Charles's old house?"

"Yeah, that's the one."

"It might be more money than you wanted to spend," Sam said. "We're asking three hundred thousand for it. So that's what we're putting it on the market for."

Charlie Gardner whistled. "That's pretty salty. Of course, if it were just me, I'd be happy in the house we bought. It's your mother. She really liked Olive's house."

"It is a beautiful house," Sam said. "Which is why it's so expensive."

"There ought to be a way we can swing it. Maybe you could ask the meeting to lower the price a little since we're your parents."

"Dad, I can't do that," Sam said. "It wouldn't be appropriate."

"Oh, I'm not talking a lot. I think we could swing two hundred for it."

"So you want me to go to the meeting and ask them to give you a hundred-thousand-dollar discount?"

"Well, don't say it out like that. Just tell them you've had an offer on the house and that you think they should take it."

"And you don't think they'll want to know how much the offer was for and who made it?" Sam asked. "Dad, if you want the house, go to the trustees and make them a serious offer. But you shouldn't expect a discount just because I'm the pastor."

Charlie Gardner snorted. "What good does it do to have a son who's a minister if he won't help his own parents? This is no way to treat your mom and dad, that's all I can say."

When Sam was ten years old, he had helped his dad put a new roof on their garage. His father had lost his balance, caught his foot on the gutter, and fallen to the ground, smacking his head on the bricks bordering the flowerbed. Though his father had brushed himself off and returned to work, Sam suspected something had been dislodged, some part of the brain necessary for rational thought, for ever since then, in unpredictable moments, Charlie Gardner had acted most peculiarly.

"Dad," Sam said, as sincerely and patiently as he could, "if the house were mine, I would be happy to make you a deal on it, but the house isn't mine. It belongs to the meeting."

"And you are its pastor," his father said.

"Which is why it would be inappropriate for me to ask for special consideration."

"Well, that's a fine how-do-you-do. A man puts his son through college and seminary, only to ask one favor and be turned down flat."

Memory was interesting. When Sam had gone to college,

his parents had been unable to help him, though ever since then his father had taken credit for putting Sam through college, saying, when the subject of Sam's education arose, "We had to scrimp and save, but I'm so grateful your mother and I were able to send you to college." Sometimes Sam wondered if his dad had fallen off the garage roof more than once.

Sam decided to take a break, slipped on his jacket, and invited his sons to go for a walk around town, visiting their old haunts. It was overcast, and Sam was depressed that his sons were grown and gone, and mad at himself for not moving to California after seminary and raising his sons among the redwoods and becoming an Episcopalian priest or a writer or following some other exotic vocation, instead of coming back to a town where bagels were considered suspiciously French and people who drove Japanese cars were made to feel traitorous.

"Boys," he told them, as they walked past the Coffee Cup, "get your education and get out of Indiana. Move to Vermont or Oregon or California. Your mom and I will follow you."

"I thought you liked Indiana," Addison said. "You always told us it was the best state in America."

"I spoke too soon," Sam said.

"Are Grandma and Grandpa driving you crazy?" Levi asked.

"Yep, pretty much."

"They are me, too," Addison said. "They keep rubbing my head. How much longer do we have to stay?"

"We're going home today," Sam announced.

"I thought we were staying through the weekend," Levi said.

"Boys, if we don't leave now, we'll never leave. We'll be stuck here the rest of our lives, down in my parents' basement sorting through their stuff."

They looped past the meetinghouse. The door was unlocked, so they went in.

"I never liked this place," Levi said, standing in the meeting-room. "Dale Hinshaw was such a jerk to us."

"I'm sorry," Sam said. "If it helps any, Dale Hinshaw was a jerk to everyone. But there were nice people here, too. Miriam and Ellis, Jessie and Asa, Deena Morrison, the Grants. They're good people."

"Somebody should have punched Dale Hinshaw when he was a kid," Levi said.

"Maybe someone did," Sam said. "Maybe that's why he's the way he is."

"That's what my sergeant in basic training said," Addison said. "That the people who cause the most hurt in the world were hurt themselves."

That was a shock to Sam. When Addison had left for the military, Sam had expected him to return home a barbarian.

They stood in the silence, thinking.

"Maybe Grandpa can't get rid of anything because he didn't have anything when he was a kid," Levi suggested.

"Maybe so," Sam said. "Maybe so."

35

They stayed through the weekend, working well into the evening hours, and by Sunday noon had most of the house packed. By then Sam had talked his parents into hiring a moving company by pointing out it would take twenty pickup loads to haul their belongings to Hope, and the cost of gas would be twice as much as the cost of hiring movers.

"Didn't think of that," Charlie Gardner admitted.

They skipped meeting. The thought of spending the morning with Dale Hinshaw was more than they could bear. Sam, Barbara, and the boys made their escape after Sunday dinner, their last meal in Sam's childhood home. His mom made Sam's favorite lunch—grilled cheese and tomato soup. The dishes had been packed, so they used paper plates and drank the soup from Styrofoam cups.

They loaded their car and were on the road by two o'clock, heading north toward Hope. An hour out of town, Sam's cell phone rang. It was Wanda Fink. "Where were you this morning?" she demanded.

"I had the Sunday off, Wanda. My son is home on leave

and we were at my parents' home for Christmas, helping them move."

"We needed you here. Before church Hank Withers took all the men outside and showed them where a new addition would go. He's got it marked with stakes and everything. We haven't even decided what we're gonna do with the money and he's already got it spent."

"Wanda, if Hank wants to talk about an addition, I can't make him stop. I've told him the meeting will have to discern together what to do and he said he understood."

"Meanwhile my nephew might have to come home because no one is willing to support his ministry," Wanda complained. "Five percent! Five percent! And you're not doing the first thing about it."

"What's five percent?" Sam asked. "And how can I do anything about it, if I don't know what you're talking about?"

"That's how many Norwegians go to church," Wanda snapped. "Five percent. And you haven't lifted a finger to help."

When Wanda had first raised the subject of her nephew's work as a missionary, Sam had suspected he'd be blamed if it flopped, and sure enough, the decline of Christianity in the Nordic region was being placed squarely on his shoulders.

"Wanda, I'm driving now and it's not safe to talk. I suggest you attend our next business meeting and share your concerns there." But even as Sam advised her to attend the meeting, he prayed she wouldn't. A useless prayer, since she'd attended every church meeting since the dawn of time. Meetings were bad enough without malcontents present, blasting away at every proposal not their own.

"So I'll see you later," Sam said, clicking off his phone, not waiting for her response.

"Wanda Fink?" Barbara asked.

"None other."

Barbara sighed. "That woman is a red-hot mess."

When Sam pulled into the meetinghouse lane an hour later, Wanda was in the meetinghouse yard, pulling up the stakes Hank had placed, tossing them aside in a mad frenzy. Sam left her to it. He had spent the past week arguing with elderly people set in their ways and was in no mood to do it again.

There were seven messages on their answering machine, all of them from people in the meeting, asking Sam to return their call at the first opportunity. Sam listened to them, deleting them as he went.

"Aren't you going to call them?" Barbara asked.

"Not today," Sam said. "I'm on vacation. And tomorrow is my day off. So on Tuesday morning, when I arrive at my office, I will phone them. But not until then."

They made pizza for supper and played Monopoly at the kitchen table. Sam was a whiz with play money. It was a mystery to Barbara how Sam could end up with hotels on every property and enough five-hundred-dollar bills to gag a horse, but couldn't balance a checkbook to save his soul. Barbara was the first to declare bankruptcy, having loaned her children money like the loving mother she was. Then Levi landed on Park Place, owed Sam 1,500 dollars, and went belly-up. Addison flamed out on the next roll and Sam declared himself the Donald Trump of Quakerism and spent the rest of the evening being obnoxious.

Sam and Barbara went to bed a little before midnight. Addison and Levi stayed up to talk brother talk. Sam and Barbara lay awake listening to their sons laugh.

"Remember when they were little and fought all the time and we worried they wouldn't like each other when they grew up?" Sam said.

"Yes. I love hearing them talk to one another. It's my favorite sound in the world."

Before long Barbara fell asleep. She was a light snorer. Sam listened to her, the in-and-out breathing with the slightest trumpet ruffles. After a while he heard the boys go to bed, saying good night to each other, then Addison saying to Levi, "Love you, Brother." And Levi, surprised at first, then finding his voice. "Love you, too, man. It's been good seeing you."

Sam thought of Art Drucker and his wife and three sons, whom Sam remembered slightly. It had been a long time ago. Over forty years. Sam wondered what had become of the boys and thought maybe he'd look them up on Facebook, but couldn't remember their first names.

Art Drucker had given everything up—lying beside his wife and talking late into the night, watching his sons grow up to enjoy one another. Tossed it aside to run off with Nate Griffith's wife, who wasn't all that nice from what Sam could remember. Kind of a scrawny, pinched-up woman with stringy hair and yellowed fingertips from smoking. When she'd gotten saved, she'd stayed pinched up, but had quit smoking and, having stopped, harangued to death anyone who hadn't.

Then Sam thought of Gretchen Weber and her French braid for a while. There were times Sam had impure thoughts, which he believed were normal, he being a man and Gretchen Weber having a French braid. But leave Barbara and the boys for a French braid? No way on earth. Not on your life. Before long his sons would marry and along would come grandchildren, if he was lucky. He was glad to be over Gretchen, so he wouldn't end up like Art Drucker.

Sam suspected Art Drucker never knew his grandchildren, that he was never talked about after he left. Maybe thought of from time to time, but with great bitterness. He imagined Art Drucker sitting in his apartment above Owen Stout's office on Thanksgiving and Christmas Day. Maybe opening a can of soup for dinner, watching the parades on television, waiting for his phone to ring, though it never did. All because Nate Griffith spilled chicken gravy on his suit at a funeral dinner and his wife couldn't get the stain out. She'd taken the suit to Art's One-Hour Cleaners and there Art had been, bored, ready for a thrill. Sam wondered how many marriages had been ruined by gravy. It paid to eat carefully, Sam thought, as he drifted off to sleep.

36

He woke at seven, when their telephone rang. It was Ruby Hopper, phoning to tell him there had been trouble at meeting the day before. Could he meet to talk?

"How about eight o'clock?" he asked, hoping to get the meeting out of the way before the boys got going on their day.

"See you then," Ruby said.

She pulled down the meetinghouse lane just as Sam left the house, walking on the brick path over to the meetinghouse.

They greeted each other and Sam unlocked the door, nudged the thermostat up to sixty-eight degrees, then welcomed Ruby into his office.

"So what happened?" he asked.

"Wanda Fink stood during the silence and went off on Hank Withers. She called him a snake in the grass. Then she accused the rest of us of not being Christian. It was dreadful. We had four new visitors, worship had started out so beautifully, Libby Woodrum brought a wonderful message, and then Wanda went on the attack."

"Did anyone challenge her?" Sam asked.

"We were too dumbstruck to do anything. No one said a word."

"Has she ever done this before?" Sam asked.

"No. She has sometimes been a bit abrasive, but never during worship. It was entirely inappropriate."

"It's only going to get worse when we have the money in hand," Sam predicted. "Then it will be much more real."

"I know Olive meant well, but I'm beginning to wish she had never given us that money. It's caused nothing but trouble."

Sam dreaded what they had to do next, but it couldn't be avoided. "Let's go over to the Finks' house and talk with Wanda. We have to stop this nonsense right now."

They took Ruby's car, and found Wanda and Leonard still in their bathrobes, eating breakfast. Pancakes. Sam loved pancakes.

"Those smell delicious," he said, hoping for an invitation to breakfast, but one was not forthcoming.

"I suppose you're here to lecture me about yesterday," Wanda said.

"We did want to speak with you about that, yes," Ruby said. "But we should have phoned first. Would you be available to talk later today?"

"You're here now. You might as well get it over with," Wanda said.

"May we sit?" Ruby asked with a smile.

It appeared Ruby was taking the lead, which suited Sam just fine.

Wanda nodded toward the chairs.

"Wanda, first we just want to say we understand your frustration," Ruby said. "Hank is obviously very excited about the possibilities available to us now, as we all are. In his enthusiasm, he is running a bit ahead of the meeting."

"Then why aren't you over at his house at eight fifteen in the morning lecturing him?" Wanda snapped.

"Ruby has every intention of talking with Hank, too," Sam said, deftly laying that task in Ruby's lap.

"I should hope so," said Leonard Fink.

"Hank will be spoken to at the proper time," Ruby said, "but this morning I want to address your behavior in yesterday's meeting for worship. It is never appropriate to use worship to air one's grievances, or to call someone a name, or to denigrate the Christian commitment of other people. Wanda, you have been a member of our meeting for many years and we love you, but your conduct yesterday was inappropriate."

Crisp, clear, to the point. It was as fine an eldering as Sam had ever seen, and it made Wanda furious.

"I don't suppose it would have occurred to you that I was led by God to say the things I did," Wanda said.

Ruby sat quietly for a moment, her eyes closed, her hands folded in her lap.

"Your words didn't feel as if they came from God," Ruby said finally, her voice soft. "We felt no love in them."

"God doesn't always speak with love," Wanda said. "Read your Bible. God also speaks with judgment and anger."

"I felt nothing of the Spirit in your words," Ruby said. "God is love. When people claim to speak for God, there should be love in their words. Besides, we've only just begun this discussion. Let's not escalate to anger so quickly. Let's be patient with one another and bring our best selves to this situation, not our worst."

Her words resonated with Wanda, whose countenance softened. "Perhaps I did speak too harshly. But when I saw those stakes in the yard, as if we had already decided to build on without having discussed it, it upset me."

"It troubled me also," Ruby conceded. She turned to Sam. "Had Hank spoken to you about placing those stakes? He was under the impression you'd asked him to do that to give us an idea of the addition he had in mind."

"I simply suggested that he and Wilson Roberts and Wayne Newby make a presentation to the meeting so we could better understand what they had in mind. I asked them to include Dan Woodrum, so he would feel a part of things. The next thing I knew, Hank and Wayne were setting stakes in the meetinghouse lawn."

Sam didn't hesitate to throw Hank Withers under the bus. If Hank had been more patient, this would never have happened.

"How come I wasn't included?" Leonard asked. "I've been going to the meeting a lot longer than Dan Woodrum. He's not even a member. As far as I'm concerned, he shouldn't have a say in the meeting's business."

Leonard Fink was a sniveler.

"Yes, Leonard never gets invited to do anything with the other men in the church. They never invite him to lunch. If there's a meeting, they don't include him. Why is that?" Wanda demanded.

Sam almost said it was because Leonard was a pain in the butt and none of the guys really liked him, then remembered he was a minister, so lied instead. "I'm sure it's not intentional. The men of the church think a great deal of Leonard."

He and Ruby stayed a bit longer, thanked Wanda and Leonard for their selfless dedication to the meeting, then scurried away before the Finks got wound up about something else.

"Are we going to talk with Hank?" Sam asked, as they pulled out of the Finks' driveway.

"We are not, you are," Ruby Hopper said. "Don't think I didn't notice you putting that off on me."

"I think it would go over better coming from you," Sam said. "I read once where men respond better to women than they do to other men. Not that I mind talking with him. I'm just thinking of what's best for the meeting."

Ruby thought for a moment. "Maybe there's something to what you're saying. Perhaps he'll feel a bit less threatened if I speak with him."

"I couldn't agree more," Sam said happily.

The day was turning out fine after all. It wasn't yet nine o'clock, Wanda Fink had been set straight, and Sam had the rest of the day with his family. It was no wonder he enjoyed ministry so much.

37

The rest of the day flew past. Levi's girlfriend, Monica, came over, Sam built a fire in the fireplace, and Barbara made brownies. After lunch Addison set Barbara's laptop computer on the kitchen table and Skyped his Mormon girlfriend, who was at home with her family in Nevada. They seemed nice enough, though Sam remained a bit leery of Mormons, having been let down by their underwear. Then, as he talked with Addison's girlfriend and discovered Mormons had no paid clergy, that those who worked in the church were expected to donate their time, he became downright appalled, and determined then and there never to become a Mormon.

"Boy, I hope word of that never gets out," Sam told Barbara, after they'd finished Skyping.

When Barbara pointed out that many Quaker meetings had no paid clergy, Sam was not appeased.

"I am well aware of that," he told her, "but don't you think that could become a dangerous trend?"

"Hmm, let's see, churches not paying mostly males to stand

up front and tell everyone else what to think and what to do?" Barbara said. "Gee, that would be horrible."

"Yes, that would be terrible, wouldn't it?" Monica said. "How would we poor, dumb laypeople ever know what to do without a big, strong male minister telling us?"

The women began to snort, laughing.

Barbara was growing fond of Monica.

For supper Sam cooked hamburgers on the grill, then after supper they watched a movie about an alien life force that attempted to take over the United States and would have succeeded, had it not picked on a family of hillbillies armed to the teeth, who had the aliens shot, skinned, and tacked out on the side of a barn within a half hour.

"Moral of the story, don't ever make a hillbilly mad," Sam said.

Sam and his sons were in agreement that it was the best movie they had seen in years, while Barbara and Monica had given up ten minutes into it and retreated to the basement to watch a movie about a man dying of a rare disease after being bitten by a mouse in Mexico. He fell in love with his infectious disease doctor, a bright, beautiful woman who had graduated from Harvard Medical School the year before. They were married in his hospital room an hour before he expired. The movie showed the couple on their honeymoon, in the hospital bed, the man in tears, the woman consoling him, urging him to be brave, that it wasn't the end of the world, even though it was for him. As it turned out, the man was insured for ten million dollars, which went to his new wife, who paid off her college loans, bought a house, and married another doctor.

"I just love a happy ending," Monica said.

"Don't you, though," Barbara said.

They both agreed it was the best movie they had seen in years.

That night, it being New Year's Eve, they turned on the television and watched the ball drop in Times Square, then went to bed. Monica stayed the night, sleeping on the new air mattress in the living room.

Sam and Barbara lay awake, a bit too wound up to sleep.

"Sam, if I ask you a question, will you tell me the truth?"

"Of course."

"One of the teachers said she saw you at Bruno's eating lunch with another woman. I know you have lunch sometimes with people in the church, but she made it sound like it wasn't one of the women from the meeting."

"It was Gretchen Weber," Sam said, spilling his guts. "She came in while I was having lunch and sat down with me. I had a dream about her, too. Is it cheating if you dream about someone else?"

"What kind of dreams?"

"Dreams a married man shouldn't have about another woman."

"I don't suppose we can help our dreams," Barbara said. "But we can help who we have lunch with. You might be a bit more careful."

"I didn't plan it. It just happened."

"Just be careful," Barbara said. "People gossip." She turned to look at Sam. "You're not going to leave me, are you?"

"Not in a million years," Sam promised. "You won't leave me, will you?"

"Only if you keep having lunches with that little hussy."

"Never again. I won't even see her."

"Oh, Sam. You're bound to see her. She lives in the area, she's related to Ruby. She comes to meeting from time to time. She even seems nice. Just keep your wits about you and don't give people a reason to talk."

"I won't," Sam said. He scooted closer to Barbara. "Want to snuggle?"

"Nope."

"Didn't think so. Are you mad?"

"No, Sam. Just don't be stupid, okay?"

"I won't be," he promised. "I don't want to lose you."

Barbara fell asleep, but Sam stayed wide awake, for fear he would dream about Gretchen and ruin his marriage.

38

The males made breakfast the next morning, New Year's
Day—Cocoa Krispies, bananas, and orange juice.

"Well, today's the big day," Sam announced during breakfast. "Mom and Dad are moving."

His parents had already phoned three times that morning,
making sure Sam would be at their new home to welcome the
movers.

"If they're not there by five o'clock, it means they've stolen
our furniture," his dad said. "Call the police."

"Dad, I don't think they'll steal your furniture."

"I've got some valuable stuff in that truck. You never know
what someone might do. Five o'clock. On the dot. If they're
not there, call the cops. Promise?"

"Yes, Dad, I promise."

In the background Sam heard his mother say, "I'm sure
the police department will send out the helicopters and the
SWAT team to find your antique wrench collection."

"Your mother has been driving me crazy. She's always after
me to throw perfectly good things away. Just throw them away,
like they were trash!"

Sam's mother picked up the extension. "Sam, I know you're busy and that you have a job and Addison is home and you want to spend time with him, but we're going to need you for the next week or so. Will you be able to help us unpack our boxes and put things away?"

"Mom, I'll do what I can," Sam promised. "We might not get it all done this week, but we'll keep chipping away at it."

"You know your father. He'll be absolutely no help at all. He'll get distracted with something and nothing will get done."

"I'm sure everything will work out just fine," Sam said.

"Your father will be the death of me. He has all these grand ideas, but sticks me with all the work."

"I can hear what you're saying about me," Sam's father said. "I'm not deaf."

Sam suspected this would be his future, his parents phoning each day so he could listen to them bicker with one another.

"We'll see you later today. Love you both. Be safe," Sam said, then hung up the phone.

Technically Sam was supposed to work, but it was New Year's Day, so he spent it with his family instead. Addison regaled them with stories of army life, a world foreign to them. Sam didn't think he would have made it in the military. He had never been good at following orders, and hated conflict of any sort. The idea of gouging someone's eyeball out or kneeing them in the crotch made him nauseous, plus he hated the sight of blood, especially his own.

Levi launched into a college story about a guy in his dorm who'd drunk so much beer he'd fallen out a window and would have died, except that it was on the first floor and he'd landed in a bush.

"But this semester he's moving to a room on the sixth floor

and if he falls from there it'll pretty well kill him," Levi said, as if he couldn't wait to see it.

At three they drove Monica home, where they met her parents and exchanged pleasantries. Her mother and Sam kvetched about working for the church, working up a good head of steam, until Barbara reminded Sam they needed to leave in order to be on time to meet his parents' moving van.

"Yeah, my parents bought a house right down the street from us," Sam said.

"I'm so sorry," Monica's mother said. "I can't imagine."

"Plus, they're going to join the Quaker meeting I pastor," Sam added.

"It goes from bad to worse," she said.

Levi was uncertain whether to kiss Monica good-bye in front of everyone, so shook her hand instead, and the Gardners took their leave to meet the movers.

39

Sam's phone rang promptly at five o'clock.

"Are they there yet?"

"Not yet, Dad. We're still waiting."

Sam had dropped Barbara and the boys off at their house and was now seated in the car across the street from his parents' new home, waiting for the movers to arrive.

"Hang up and call the police," his father ordered.

"Dad, I'm not going to call the police. The movers probably stopped to get a bite to eat."

"I told them not to. We need that truck unpacked today. I told them not to dillydally."

In the background Sam could hear his mother. "Ask Sam if we can eat meals at their house this week. I won't have my kitchen set up yet."

"We'll be eating at your house this week," his father said. "Your mother's not able to cook yet."

"Dad, I don't think that will work. But there are lots of affordable restaurants in the area, so you won't go hungry."

"What? You think we're made of money? We can't afford to eat out every meal. Are they there yet?"

"No, not yet," Sam said.

"That's it. I'm calling the police. I knew this would happen. They're probably in Kansas by now."

"Dad, call the movers, give them my cell number, and tell them to call me when they get here."

Sam left for home.

A police officer phoned fifteen minutes later to ask Sam what he knew about the theft of his parents' furniture.

"We don't know that anything has been stolen," Sam explained. "The movers probably stopped to eat supper. My father gets impatient."

"We have to investigate," the officer explained, "unless, of course, your father lacks sufficient mental capacity and might have mistakenly reported this."

"He's nuttier than a fruitcake," Sam said.

"Call us first thing tomorrow if you haven't heard from the moving company. Some of these guys are con artists. They steal a truck, load it up, and have the furniture sold within the hour."

Sam had no sooner hung up than his father phoned to ask if the moving van had arrived.

"I don't know, Dad. I'm at my house. Did you try calling them?"

"Yes, a voice came on and said the number wasn't in service."

"What was the name of the moving company?" Sam asked.

"Their company didn't have a name. I saw their ad on the bulletin board down at the McDonald's by the interstate. There were three of them. They said they were from Cartersburg. They said they knew you. That's why I hired them."

"They said they knew me? What were their names?"

"One of them was named Jim."

"Jim who?"

"I didn't catch his last name, but he said he knew you."

Sam could hear his mother in the background, weeping. "All our family pictures were on that truck. And my mother's china."

"Maybe their truck broke down," Sam said. "Let's not get all worked up yet. When will you and Mom be here?"

"Not for another few hours."

"I bet they'll be here and have half the truck unloaded by then," Sam said, even though he suspected they had sold off the whole shebang and were at that moment snorting cocaine up their thieving noses. "Come here first. You can spend the night with us."

His mother and father pulled down the meetinghouse lane a little before nine, the truck still hadn't arrived, and his mom and dad were fit to be tied.

"Why would a friend of yours do this to us?" Sam's mother asked him.

"Mom, there could be a perfectly reasonable explanation. Maybe their truck broke down. And just because someone says they know me, doesn't mean they do. Maybe they told you that to get on your good side. It might have been a lie."

"It seems to me you should use a little better judgment picking your friends," his father said.

"I don't even know this man," Sam said. "You chose him, not me."

"Because he said you were friends."

"Again, he might have been saying that to con you. This is what happens when you hire someone without references."

They phoned the movers again, with no luck, and finally

went to bed around midnight. The next morning Sam walked down to the house. No movers. He phoned the police department to report the furniture stolen. They returned his call around noon to report the truck had been found parked behind a barn ten miles south of Harmony, near Cartersburg. A farmer had noticed it and called the police.

"We need to keep the truck," the police officer explained. "But if you can identify your belongings, we'll be happy to turn them over to you. You'll need to bring a truck."

Sam left his parents with Barbara and took Levi and Addison with him, stopping on the way to rent a U-Haul. It took them several hours to transfer the belongings from one truck to another. The television set was missing, and the antique wrench collection was nowhere to be found, but the family picture albums were still there, along with the china. Otherwise the thieves had done an excellent job packing the truck and securing the contents, which Sam thought spoke well of them.

"Boy, that was an awful lot of work for a TV and a bunch of old wrenches," Levi said.

"Just goes to show crime doesn't pay," Sam said.

They drove back to Hope and unloaded the U-Haul. They carried off the couch first. His father collapsed on it, bemoaning the loss of his beloved wrenches. Gloria Gardner, grateful the pictures and china had been recovered, stood in their new living room, directing the operation, like Eisenhower on D Day. By nine o'clock the truck had been unloaded and returned, and they were sitting down to dinner, takeout from Bruno's. Salads and lasagna and garlic rolls. Charles Gardner had revived and was making plans for the future.

"I was getting kind of tired of collecting wrenches anyway. I'm thinking maybe now that I got that big backyard, I can go back to collecting tractors." He turned to Sam. "Did you know in 1951, there were five hundred and sixty-four thousand tractors made right here in America?"

"I had no idea," Sam said.

"Yep, five hundred and sixty-four thousand tractors in 1951," Charlie Gardner repeated, awed by the wonder of it. "Of course we'll have to get the backyard cleaned up first. When can you and the boys do that? How about tomorrow? Shouldn't take more than two or three days, if you hit it hard."

Six feet, Sam thought. *If I bury him at least six feet down, no one should ever find him.*

40

They drove Addison to the airport the next day and said their good-byes, then drove home in silence, already missing him. As they pulled down the meetinghouse lane, it began to rain, sheets of water streaming down for two days, as if God had knocked over a bucket.

Sam and Barbara spent the next two evenings at his parents' new home, helping them organize, while his father prattled on about tractors.

On the third day, Wilson Roberts and Ruby Hopper came to clean the meetinghouse, which was when Wilson first noticed water on the floor in the men's restroom.

"At first I thought the toilet was leaking," he told Ruby, "but I put that toilet in myself, so I figured it couldn't be that, then I looked up and sure enough the ceiling was stained."

He phoned Sam, who called Hank Withers, who came with his ladder and inspected the roof, poking and prodding, before climbing down to announce that Wayne Newby had done such an exceptional job making the roof look hail-damaged that it was, in fact, ruined, and not just leaking into the men's restroom, but also into the women's restroom, utility closet, kitchen, and nursery.

"Basically, the whole roof is shot," Hank said. "Thanks to Wayne Newby. I'm surprised the ceiling hasn't collapsed. There's probably all kinds of water trapped up there."

Hank went home and returned a half hour later with buckets and a screwdriver duct-taped to the end of a broom handle. He went from room to room, poking holes in the ceiling to let the water drain into the buckets he'd placed on the floor.

"That's pretty smart," Sam said.

"Easier to patch a hole than it is to replace a ceiling," Hank said. "But we're going to have to pull out the insulation and replace it. Dang that Wayne Newby anyway."

With the water draining, Hank began working the office phone, phoning the members of the roof committee for an emergency meeting. They were all there within a half hour, assembled in Sam's office. They spent the first half hour ripping into Wayne, who wasn't there to defend himself, even entertaining the notion of excommunication, until Sam reminded them they were Christians and supposed to forgive people even if they were stupid.

"Sam's right," Wilson Roberts said. "Complaining about Wayne isn't going to get the roof fixed. Meanwhile, we're supposed to get more rain this weekend. We've got to get that roof covered."

The committee piled into Wilson's Cadillac, several of them commenting on what a fine car it was and how they'd always wanted one, but that it didn't seem very Quakerly to be driving around in a Cadillac when so many people were in need.

"I'm a Chevy man myself," Leonard Fink said. "But I suppose if a man can live with himself, then a Cadillac is a fine car to drive."

They pulled up to Riggle's Hardware, trooped in, and purchased every tarp in the store, then drove back to the meetinghouse and covered the entire roof in bright blue plastic, like a Mississippi trailer.

"That looks god-awful," Hank Withers said, standing on the meetinghouse lawn surveying their work. "How soon can we get a new roof?"

"I guess when Olive's estate gets settled and we get a check," Sam said. "Unless someone wants to donate a new roof or loan us the money." He looked around at the roof committee, hoping one of the members might step up and say, "I'll buy a new roof, and don't worry about paying me back." But no one did.

"Looks like we better get used to having a blue roof," Sam said.

"Maybe we can have a fund-raiser and draw one of those big thermometers and color it in as we get the money," Wilson suggested. "That's what we do in the Rotary Club."

"Maybe we can cut down one of our oak trees and make some shingles the way they used to, out of oak shakes, and put it on ourselves," Hank said. "I saw it done on YouTube. We could get a shingle froe and a mallet and we'd be in business."

That idea sounded like a tremendous amount of work and was quickly shot down.

"You actually want us to make our own shingles from an oak tree and put them up there ourselves?" Wilson Roberts asked. "Who the hell do you think we are? Pioneers?"

"Then maybe you want to pay for a new roof," Hank said. "Because that's our only other option."

It was the general consensus of Hope Friends Meeting that Wilson Roberts was loaded to the gills, with secret bank accounts in Switzerland and the Cayman Islands, which explained the Cadillac.

"Well, I tell you one thing," Wilson said. "I'll pay for a new roof before I climb up on that roof and fall and bust my head open."

"Then it's settled," Leonard Fink said. "Wilson's donating a new roof to the meetinghouse."

"Not donating. Loaning. When we get our check from Olive's estate, the meeting can repay me."

"Fair enough," Sam said, before Wilson thought better of it. "Hank, can you line up some roofers and get going on this?"

"Wayne Newby is the head of the roof committee," Hank said. "He should be the one doing it."

"Wayne Newby!" Leonard Fink shrieked. "Wayne Newby! He's the one who got us into this mess. I say we boot him off the committee altogether."

"Let's give him a chance to redeem himself," Sam suggested. "Having caused all this trouble, he'll be anxious to make amends. Let's let him try."

Sam had recently gotten a peek at the financial records of the meeting and had discovered Wayne and Doreen Newby were the second-largest givers in the meeting, behind Wilson Roberts. It wouldn't pay to anger them.

"One more chance," Leonard Fink grumbled. "If he blows it this time, he's out of here for good."

Leonard and Wanda Fink were the lowest givers in the congregation. It had been Sam's general experience that the people who helped the least were the same ones who caused the most trouble.

"I'll call Wayne and ask him to head it up," Hank said. "Maybe we won't have to look at this blue roof all winter long."

Sam shook hands with Wilson Roberts. "Thanks for the loan, Wilson. We appreciate it."

Sam was impressed by their progress. If this had happened at Harmony Friends Meeting, there would have been a dozen committee meetings and a study of pertinent Scripture with Dale Hinshaw asking them to consider 1 Kings 6:9—*So he built the temple and completed it, roofing it with beams and cedar planks.* Which would have led to a spirited debate about cedar versus asphalt shingles, and a long drawn-out lecture by one of the trustees on the history of roofing materials.

All things considered, Sam felt good about the day, even with the meetinghouse roof covered in plastic.

41

The meeting was spared from having to borrow money from Wilson Roberts when Jack Shear, the attorney for Olive's estate, appeared the next morning at the meetinghouse to inform Sam that due to his own unflagging efforts Olive's estate had been settled and the meeting would have its check the following Monday.

"Eight hundred and twenty-three thousand dollars and fifty-two cents. My fees came to fifteen thousand dollars. The judge okayed it and I've already been paid. Fifty hours at three hundred dollars an hour. You'll find that's quite typical."

It seemed outrageous to Sam, who had been to college a year more than Jack Shear and would have happily sat through church meetings all day long if someone were paying him three hundred dollars an hour to do so.

"The transfer of the house is a bit more complicated, but we should have that wrapped up within the week," he assured Sam.

After Jack Shear left, Sam sat at his desk, getting accustomed to the feeling of wealth. He'd never pastored a meeting with that kind of loot. Eight hundred and twenty-three thousand dollars! Somewhere in that pile of money was a raise for him. He rummaged around his desk for a calculator. Invested on the stock market for a conservative 7 percent yearly return, almost fifty-eight thousand dollars a year. Unless they sent the money to Wanda's missionary nephew or added on to the meetinghouse. He didn't need the entire fifty-eight thousand. Twenty of it would do nicely, leaving the congregation with thirty-eight thousand dollars a year to spend on other things. They could throw Wanda's nephew a bone, borrow the money for an addition, and make the monthly nut from the interest earned. Sometimes Sam thought maybe he should have worked on Wall Street.

Barbara was still on break from school, so he walked over to the parsonage and told her his idea. She stared at him, astounded. "You actually think a Quaker meeting is going to give its pastor a twenty-thousand-dollar raise? Have you been drinking?"

"I've got it all figured out. They have the money."

"It's not about the church having the money, Sam. It's about custom and tradition. Quaker ministry has never paid much, and that isn't going to change just because a Quaker meeting has money. They'll bank it and spend the interest on service projects. You watch and see."

"What about the addition?" Sam asked. "Do you think they'll do that?"

"Build on an addition for a church with twenty people? Nope, I'm betting they won't do that, either."

"Hank Withers isn't going to like that," Sam predicted.

"I have a feeling no one is going to be completely satisfied no matter what we do."

Sam thought for a moment and decided she was probably right, which left him in such a funk he almost forgot to call Ruby Hopper to tell her Olive's estate had been settled.

Ruby's reaction was somewhat guarded. "I must be honest. While I appreciate Olive's generosity, I'm not looking forward to the discussions we'll be having about this money. I spoke with Hank about backing off of the building addition, but he's insistent. Says if we don't need it now, we'll need it in the future. Then he said he was tired of Wanda Fink being so bossy and always getting her way and that he wasn't going to put up with it anymore."

"You think we can get him settled down?" Sam asked.

"I don't know. He was pretty upset."

"You know Hank a lot better than I do, but this doesn't seem like him."

"It isn't like him," Ruby said. "But ever since Norma was diagnosed with Alzheimer's, he angers easily."

"Maybe the meeting should consult with a financial advisor," Sam suggested. "Or maybe there's an organization somewhere that advises nonprofits on finances. You want me to start doing a little research?"

"That's a wonderful idea, Sam. Why don't you do that? Don't commit to anything, but if we could present several options to the congregation, it might be helpful."

Sam walked back to his office, went on Google, entered the keywords "rich" and "church," and was directed to the website of a pastor in Tennessee who had written a diatribe, in capital letters, against rich churches, how God would spew them out of his mouth. There were several citations from the book of Revelation and a prediction of everlasting torment.

He returned to Google and entered the words "financial

management for churches." There were twenty-three million hits, so he typed the words "how should churches spend their money" and dropped to fifteen million hits, which was heading in the right direction, but still too many. Nevertheless he clicked on a few of the websites and began reading about churches that had been zipping along, doing just fine, loving and serving, then someone gave them a boatload of money and they turned on one another like rabid jackals.

"It was the worst thing that ever happened to us," wrote B. K. Ritchie, a Baptist pastor from Georgia. "Things came to a head at a church meeting, when one of our deacons pulled a gun and started shooting people."

Yes, Sam could see how that might put a damper on things.

He phoned a few financial advisors, all of whom expected to be paid for their services. Sam knew that wouldn't fly. There were always two or three people in every church who considered themselves financial wizards, who wouldn't dream of paying someone for advice they were perfectly capable of figuring out on their own. Sam could hear them now. "What do you mean, we got to pay that fella five thousand dollars? We're paying him money? He ought to pay us money. It won't cost us anything to buy a CD. Sure, we might not make as much, but we won't lose anything, either. I'll tell you what this fancy-pants finance guy will do, he'll throw it in the stock market, which to me is no different from gambling and something the church shouldn't be involved in to start with."

So the church would put the money in a certificate of deposit, and once a month, for the next fifty years, the treasurer would stand at the monthly business meeting and proudly announce their investment had earned them three dollars that month. People would absorb the news quietly, then someone would say, "That doesn't sound like much, but don't forget we're earning that every month. Why, after fifty years, that's"—he (it was always a he) would pause to figure the numbers in his head—"that's almost two thousand dollars, which is some serious money."

No, there was no use even bringing up the subject of a financial advisor. Who did they think they were, anyway? Charging people for advice that many people happily offered for free.

Eight hundred and twenty-three thousand dollars in the bank, plus the money from the sale of Olive's house, plus a 1979 Ford Granada with good rubber. Let the storm hit. They were ready.

42

Gretchen Weber, her hair in a French braid, came to meeting for worship the next Sunday with her aunt Ruby. Sam greeted her, even shaking her hand, but only briefly, then worked Barbara into the conversation, just in case Gretchen had any ideas. He wondered if people shared dreams. If someone dreamed about someone else, did that someone else have the same dream? He thought maybe they did, because after worship, while everyone was eating pie, Gretchen sat beside him and talked with him about pie, which she had to know was his favorite subject.

"Maybe I'll make you a pie sometime," she said.

Sam felt his resistance melting.

"She makes wonderful pies," Ruby Hopper said. "Though I don't like admitting it, they're even better than mine."

What is it with Ruby Hopper? Sam wondered. *She's practically begging me to have an affair.*

Sam glanced around the room, looking for Barbara. She was seated with the Woodrums. Their daughter, Janet, was visiting that weekend from Harmony. Janet was the librarian at the Harmony Public Library, having succeeded Miss Rudy, the longtime librarian. She had hired Barbara, then had suggested to her mother, Libby Woodrum, to hire Barbara to be the elementary school librarian when the Gardners moved to Hope. Barbara and Janet were deep in conversation, oblivious to Gretchen's infatuation with Sam.

"That's okay," Sam said. "I don't need a pie. I'm getting a bit of a belly. But I appreciate the thought."

"Now that I have a little more time, I've started walking every day on my lunch break," Gretchen said. "Perhaps you and Barbara could join me."

"Barbara doesn't get a very long lunch break," Sam said, looking for an out.

"Then I'll stop by the meetinghouse and pick you up," Gretchen offered. "I walk right past here anyway. It's not out of my way."

"Walking is wonderful exercise," Ruby Hopper said. "I walk two miles every day, rain or shine. Have for years. Harry Truman walked two miles every day and lived to be eighty-eight."

"My grandpa smoked like a chimney, didn't exercise a day in his life, and lived to be ninety-two," Sam said.

"Still, I imagine he would have lived even longer if he had walked every day," Ruby Hopper said. "You need to exercise, Sam."

What was it with Ruby Hopper? Was she clueless? Or naïve? Or worse, wanting Sam to kick Barbara to the curb and hook up with her niece?

Gretchen was at the office at noon the next day. Sam watched as she walked down the meetinghouse lane toward his office.

He met her at the front door. He hadn't mentioned it to Barbara, not knowing whether Gretchen would show up, not wanting to raise the subject unless it became necessary. He spent most of the walk praying he wouldn't see anyone he knew, and had made it to the last block when his father drove by and rolled to a stop alongside them.

"Hi, Dad. You remember Gretchen Weber. She was at meeting yesterday. She's Ruby Hopper's niece."

"And Miriam Hodge's niece, if I'm not mistaken," Charlie Gardner said. "You visited Harmony Meeting a few years ago. How are you, Gretchen?"

"I'm fine. Just trying to get your son a little healthier."

"Good luck with that. He's never been one for exercise."

He studied Sam, curious.

"Does Barbara know you're with another woman while she's at work?"

His father had never been one for subtlety.

"We're just walking is all," Sam said, flustered. "Nothing more."

"Oh, you better watch out for me. I have plans for you," Gretchen said, laughing. "Miriam and Ruby and I are wild women."

Was she joking? Sam wasn't sure.

Charlie Gardner chuckled. "Yeah, that Miriam is a wild one."

He drove on, and Gretchen and Sam continued their walk.

"Does being alone with me make you nervous?" Gretchen asked.

"Oh no," he said. "I'm often alone with women. Comes with the job."

"It's just that we're about the same age," Gretchen said. "And I'm not married and I might be mistaken, but I've noticed that you seem to be attracted to me. Or am I just imagining that?"

Even though it was cold outside, Sam began to sweat. Why had he gone on a walk with Gretchen Weber? What had he been thinking?

"I'm a married man," Sam said.

"That doesn't mean you can't be attracted to other women," Gretchen said.

"You're right, it doesn't. I can look at a woman and find myself attracted to her. But that doesn't mean I have to act on it. I'm able to control myself."

Was she making a pass at him, or was this a philosophical discussion? He wasn't sure.

"Are you attracted to me?" she asked.

"Well, sure. I imagine lots of guys are. But that doesn't mean anything."

How had he gotten himself in this mess? *That darn French braid*, he thought bitterly, angry with himself.

"Is this conversation making you uncomfortable?" Gretchen asked.

"No, no. I'm fine."

"I just think men and women should be honest with one another, that's all."

"Oh, I agree. Honesty is good," Sam lied. "I'm all for honesty. Yes, honesty is the best policy. I can't argue with that."

"As long as we're being honest with one another, I will say I'm attracted to you, Sam. Do you think we might spend more time together?"

Not knowing what else to do or say, and having no experience with adultery, Sam threw up a little in his mouth and wished he'd stayed home.

43

Hope Friends Meeting took possession of Olive's house the next day. Sam and Hank Withers went to the closing and Sam watched while Hank signed on behalf of Hope Friends Meeting. Jack Shear signed for the estate, then gave them three keys to the house and a stack of utility bills that had been paid since Olive's death, and offered to walk them through the house if they wished, which they didn't.

Ruby Hopper and Wilson Roberts met them at the house. They went through it together, moving from room to room. The house needed more work than they had realized. Wallpaper was hanging down in some of the rooms, the plaster was cracked, there was water damage in the kitchen, and the exterior needed painting.

The furniture was dusty, but to Sam's eye was well-built and attractive.

"We ought to hold an auction and unload this stuff," Wilson Roberts said.

"I don't know," Ruby Hopper said. "There are several antiques here, and some of these paintings might be valuable. Olive had good taste. We might do better selling the furnishings outright."

"Who'd want to buy this old junk?" Wilson Roberts said.

"It's hardly junk." Hank Withers pointed to a cherrywood cupboard in the living room. "That looks to be from the mid–eighteen hundreds and it's in pristine condition."

"Why don't we hire an appraiser to give us an estimate on these things, then see if whoever buys the house might want to buy them, too," Sam suggested. "If there's anything left over, we can decide then what to do with them."

"Maybe someone in the meeting would want to buy a piece of furniture to remember Olive by," Ruby said.

"That's fine," Sam said. "When the appraiser gives us a price, we can let them have it for that price."

"I wouldn't mind having that cupboard," Hank Withers said. "That's a beauty."

"I'm going to recommend to the meeting that we hire an appraiser and take it from there," Ruby said.

They agreed, then continued poking around the house, sticking their heads in the garage where Olive's 1979 Ford Granada resided. Hank climbed in and tried starting it, but the battery was dead. They went up in the attic, which was stuffed to the gills. They stood at the head of the stairs, staring into the detritus of Olive Charles's life.

"I saw a show on TV not long ago about this couple who moved into a house and found an old painting up in the attic and it turned out to be worth three million dollars," Wilson Roberts said. "They had set it out in the trash and a neighbor walked by and saw it, took it home and found out later how valuable it was. Sold it for three million dollars, and the couple sued him, but the judge ruled in favor of the neighbor, since the couple had thrown it away."

"And that's why we need a trained appraiser," Ruby said.

"I don't know," Wilson Roberts said. "Now that I think about it, that's just another expense we'll have to pay. I've been watching these antique shows and have a pretty good feel for this sort of thing. No sense in spending all that money when I can do it for free."

Oh, Lord, Sam thought, *it's starting.*

"Let's sleep on it," Ruby suggested, buying them some time.

They were spared the decision when, the next day, Sam received a phone call from Jack Shear, informing him that he'd been approached with an offer for the house.

"I'm not a realtor, but you don't need one to sell a house. I have a friend, another attorney, who does title work, so if the meeting accepts the offer, you can save a lot of money not having to pay a realtor."

"How much did they offer?" Sam asked.

"Two seventy-five for everything. Furnishings and car included. And they've agreed to pay all the closing costs at that price."

"I thought the house was worth three hundred thousand," Sam said.

"It's worth whatever someone is willing to pay for it. The market's been a little soft lately, and the house needs more work than I first thought. You've seen the inside. It's a little rough. The roof needs to be replaced, some of the windows are bad. Given its condition, two fifty is more than fair. So it breaks down to two fifty for the house and twenty-five for the furnishings and car. If I were you, I would take the money and not look back. Spring's coming. Before long you'll have to be mowing the yard and weeding the flowerbeds. You don't want to have to deal with that, do you?"

"No, not really. They want the car?"

"Yeah, the man saw it and got a kick out of it. It's not worth much, a couple thousand at the most."

"If they buy everything, we wouldn't have to deal with the contents, would we?" Sam asked.

"No, you wouldn't. They assume all responsibility. As is. All you have to do is show up at the closing and take their money."

"Tell you what," Sam said. "I'll run it past the meeting and get back to you. By the way, who's the couple?"

"They didn't want me to say."

"It isn't my parents, is it?"

Jack Shear chuckled. "I guess I can tell you that much. No, it isn't your parents. But the couple were hoping to hear back from the meeting by tomorrow."

Sam promised to get on it, then phoned Ruby, who began calling the members to gather their thoughts on the matter. She phoned the Finks three times, then remembered they were out of town and wouldn't be back until midweek. Everyone else advised her to sell it, even Wayne Newby, who had wanted the Granada. Ruby phoned Jack Shear that day and told him to accept the offer before the couple changed their minds.

As for Sam, he was astounded. He'd never seen a Quaker meeting move so quickly. In the space of just a few days they'd decided to replace the meetinghouse roof and sell a house, furnishings, and car, without holding hundreds of mind-numbing meetings to hash it out. At Harmony Meeting they had spent more time discussing whether or not to replace the toilet in the men's restroom.

He returned to the meetinghouse to find a Post-it note on the office door from Gretchen, asking him to call her when he returned, which he had no intention of doing, French braid or not. Instead he phoned Barbara to tell her the house had been sold, then went home and made lasagna, her favorite dish.

"The meeting now has one million, ninety-eight thousand dollars and fifty-two cents," Sam told Barbara that evening over supper. "I would be perfectly happy with a bonus of ten thousand."

"What planet are you living on?"

Even if the odds were against it, it was pleasant to think about Sam's getting a bonus, and they spent the rest of supper discussing what they might do with a big chunk of money. Barbara thought boosting their retirement fund was wise, but Sam was leaning toward a motorcycle, pointing out how much money they would save on gas. After they'd washed the supper dishes, Sam went on the Internet and read about motorcycles, scooters, golf carts, and other modes of transportation.

He woke Barbara around midnight to tell her he'd settled on an electric golf cart. "Since the church pays our utilities, we wouldn't even have to pay for the electricity. It's the same as free. Did you know they have heaters for golf carts? We could use it year-round. You could drive it to school. What do you think?"

It had long been Sam's custom to wait until Barbara was asleep before presenting her with ideas she might otherwise reject. She mumbled something in reply, he couldn't quite make it out, but thought she'd said, "That's a great idea, Sam. Let's do it."

His effort appreciated and approved, he went to bed.

He dreamed the congregation fought over the money, and

more than half the members quit, leaving seven people to soldier on. But they quickly surrendered, closed the church, and sold the meetinghouse, parsonage, and land, walking away with a quarter of a million dollars apiece. In his dream Sam and Barbara took their cut and opened a hardware store, which failed within a year, forcing them to move in with his parents. He awoke in a sweat, panicked and jittery.

"Don't ever let me open a hardware store," he told Barbara the next morning.

"Were you planning on it?"

"It's always been in the back of my mind," he admitted. "My plan B in case pastoring didn't work out."

"Then I guess you better stick with pastoring," she said. "And about that golf cart thing you mentioned last night, don't even think about it."

She climbed out of bed, pulled on her robe, and went downstairs, leaving Sam to reconsider his options.

44

~

Sam was in the office the next morning when the telephone rang. It was Gretchen, inviting him to walk with her over his lunch hour.

"I can't," he said. "It's my sermon day. And to be honest, I'm not all that comfortable being alone with you."

He had been wondering how best to tell her he wasn't interested in her and decided to be forthright.

"I don't think it's wise for us to be alone," he added.

"But I thought you were attracted to me?"

"I am. Which is why it isn't wise for us to be alone," Sam pointed out.

"Would it be all right if I made you a pie?" Gretchen asked.

"Thank you, but that's not necessary," Sam said, proud of his discipline. He had never in his life, not once ever, turned down a pie.

Sam spent the rest of the day in his office, researching a new sermon series on the afterlife, which, after his research, he wasn't sure he believed in any longer. That would certainly make for a shorter series. Maybe knock it down to one sermon with some philosophical musings and a story. Work in a few jokes. Sam had noticed you could say almost anything in a sermon so long as you told a few jokes first.

He went on the Internet to find heaven jokes, but was interrupted when he heard the front door of the meetinghouse open. He thought at first it was Gretchen, so was relieved when Wanda and Leonard Fink came into his office. It said something about his fear of Gretchen, that he preferred the company of the Finks.

"Hi, Wanda. Hi, Leonard. Is everything all right? I thought you had taken a little trip."

"Yes, that's what everyone thought, and apparently decided to wait until we were out of town before selling Olive's house without Leonard's permission," Wanda said.

Sam explained that an offer had been made, that given the house's problems it was most reasonable, and that after phoning all the members and asking their opinion on the matter they had decided to approve the sale.

"Everyone else is not a trustee of the meeting like Leonard, so it doesn't really matter whether they approve," Wanda snapped. "You need the permission of the trustees, and you didn't have it. The sale can't happen until Leonard approves it."

"But all the other trustees were in favor of it," Sam pointed out.

"I'm sure they were, but Leonard wasn't asked."

"There are five trustees. Four of them want it sold. It's unfortunate Leonard couldn't offer his opinion, but if you leave town and don't leave anyone a number where you can be reached, we can't very well ask your opinion."

"Leonard never would have approved."

"That might be, but the majority of trustees were in favor of it," Sam said.

Leonard spoke for the first time. "I don't even know why I should be a trustee if no one ever asks my opinion. I'm going to resign."

Leonard looked at Sam expectantly, waiting for Sam to talk him out of it, something Sam had no intention of doing.

"Perhaps serving as a trustee isn't your calling," Sam said diplomatically. "I heard Hank say the other day that the limb committee has an opening."

"Only idiots are on the limb committee," Wanda said. "People who are too stupid to do anything else but pick up sticks."

"Ruby Hopper is on the limb committee, as is my wife," Sam pointed out. "I'm sorry we were unable to get hold of you, but what's done is done. A good faith effort was made to contact all the trustees, they met and reached an agreement. Our word has been given, the paperwork has begun, and we're moving forward."

"I want to buy the Granada," Leonard said.

"The furnishings and car were sold with the house. It's no longer ours to sell."

"Leonard wasn't asked about that, either."

"No, Wanda, he wasn't. When we have no way of getting in touch with you, it is impossible to ask Leonard anything. Next time leave a number where you can be reached or buy a cell phone like everyone else. Now if you'll please excuse me, I have work to do."

"We're going, but this conversation isn't over," Wanda said. "Leonard's a trustee, he wasn't asked, so this is illegal. Come on, Leonard."

Nasty people, Sam thought. Any sympathy he might have felt toward their concerns was now extinguished.

He returned to his research, but could no longer concentrate, so began poking around his office, rearranging his books and cleaning his desk, then noticed the urn containing the ashes of Regina Charles. He had promised Jack Shear he would spread Regina's ashes in Olive's yard. Better to spread them before the new owners took possession. They might not like the idea of a dead person being scattered on their lawn.

It was the perfect day to scatter ashes, no wind, and not a cloud in the sky. He carried the ashes to his car and buckled them in out of habit, though the need for Regina's personal safety had long passed.

Having never scattered ashes, he was unsure of the protocol, but suspected prayer should be a part of it, so said a brief one, thanking God for Regina's life, and asking God to accept her into heaven. Though he had doubts about its existence, it never hurt to ask, just in case.

In Olive's backyard Sam found the remnants of a flowerbed beside the fence, the dried husks of shoots and blooms scrunching underfoot. He was grateful Regina had decided on cremation. Spreading her body on Olive's flowerbed wouldn't have been nearly as easy. People would have noticed. The police would have been called. There would have been questions. Not to mention the odor after her sitting in his office for a month. He scattered Regina's ashes, broadcasting them in a gentle arc among the dried flowers, watching as they settled to earth. *That's all we are*, Sam thought. *Ashes to ashes, dust to dust. We are born, we live, we die. When those who love us die, we are forgotten. Worm food.* It depressed him to think of it, so he stopped.

Now, what to do with the urn? It seemed wasteful to throw it away. It was not unattractive. It was made of porcelain and adorned with painted lilies. Quite lovely, in fact. Though the funeral director had referred to it as an urn, it was more bowl-shaped. Maybe the people who had purchased Olive's house would like it. Olive's back porch was unlocked, so he set it on a table next to the porch swing, then nosed around on the back porch, found a key to the house, and let himself in.

Technically it wasn't nosing around, since the church still owned it and he was a member of the church, which meant he was part owner. At least for now. He looked in closets and went down to the basement, inspecting the workbench and tools, most of which were rusty with age. Sam sprayed his tools with WD-40 after every use and had the shiniest tools in town, perhaps in the state.

He wandered upstairs, looking in each bedroom, opened a chest of drawers, and found Olive's underwear. Old-lady underwear with straps and buckles to hold everything in. He quickly closed the drawer. He didn't envy the person who'd have to deal with Olive's unmentionables. He pondered what would happen to his underwear after he died. Someone would have to get rid of it. His wife, probably, or maybe his sons, or a future daughter-in-law. Maybe Monica, if she and Levi married. It paid to be nice to your daughter-in-law. He was glad he had recently switched to boxers. Cleaner. Maybe if he timed it right, he could throw away his underwear right before he died, so that he ended up being buried in his last pair of skivvies. If he was cremated, would they burn his last pair of underwear with him? He wasn't sure. That would be ideal. Cremation solved so many problems.

45

Sam went by the school on his way home to see Barbara, and stuck around to read *Moose's Loose Tooth* to a group of kindergartners, who hung on his every word. He shelved a cartload of books, then talked Barbara into eating lunch with him at Bruno's, where they split a salad, an order of lasagna, and a garlic roll. He told her about the Finks and spreading Regina's ashes and poking around Olive's house.

"You shouldn't have done that," Barbara said. "That's not our house."

"Until it's sold, it's ours as much as anyone's."

"Is it nice?"

"Her tools were rusty."

After lunch he drove her back to school, then returned to his office. The light on his answering machine was blinking. Three blinks. Three missed calls. All of them from the same number. His superintendent. First the Finks, and now the superintendent. A banner day. He decided to get the pain over with as soon as possible, so called the superintendent back.

He'd phoned about the money. He'd spoken with Wanda

Fink, who had told him Olive's estate had been settled and the house sold without Leonard's consent, and that Hope Friends would soon be sitting on a million dollars they had every intention of wasting on a building program instead of using to help her nephew who was at that very moment laboring in the vineyards of the Lord, bereft and bankrupt.

"I hope the meeting has decided to obey the directive from the finance committee and give the yearly meeting its ten percent share," the superintendent said to Sam.

"From what I am able to discern thus far, that doesn't seem to be high on our list of priorities," Sam said.

"I'm disappointed to hear that."

"I think it has to do with the fact that you ignored our congregation for three years, then only showed up when we came into some money. It's caused us to doubt your sincerity," Sam pointed out.

"I was especially troubled to learn that meeting property was sold without the consent of a trustee, Leonard Fink."

"All the other trustees approved the sale. Had Leonard Fink been here, he would have sat quietly, not said a word, then gone home to his wife and told her no one asked his opinion. Then she would have griped and moaned and carried on, but it wouldn't have changed a thing. The property is being sold, the trustees approved the sale, and we're moving forward. I have work to do, so I'm going to let you go. Thank you for calling," Sam said, then hung up the phone.

Sam never tired of hanging up on the superintendent.

As for Wanda and Leonard Fink, they were starting to annoy him. He wondered if he could make them mad enough to quit. Maybe preach a sermon series on the virtues of Islam. That would get their goats. The only problem was he knew next to nothing about Islam and wasn't all that keen to learn about it. It was all he could do to keep up with Christianity. He wondered if there might be an easier way to annoy the Finks, a way that didn't involve extensive research, which he had never cared for. Maybe circulating a rumor about Leonard's cocaine habit or Wanda's sordid affair with the superintendent. That would kill two birds with one stone. Of course, none of that was true, but then that's why they were called rumors, wasn't it?

He decided to take the high road, so phoned Ruby Hopper to suggest she convene a meeting of the trustees. Cross the t's and dot the i's. Everything nice and tidy and legal.

"Let's not give anyone the opportunity to say we weren't absolutely proper," he told her. "It will give Leonard the chance to voice any concerns he might have."

"He'll sit there like a lump on a log and not say a word," Ruby said. "Then go home and complain to Wanda."

"I know that, and you know that, but at least we'll be able to say he was given the opportunity to discuss the matter."

"Yes, I suppose you're right. I'll see if the trustees can meet tonight."

So she did, and they could, so they did, and Leonard Fink didn't say the first thing, except to ask who wanted to buy Olive's house, and was told no one knew, that the couple wished to remain anonymous until the sale had been concluded, which was perfectly legal and there was nothing they could do about it.

"So you're telling me we could be selling a house to a mobster and there's nothing we can do about it," Leonard said.

The others agreed that could indeed be the case, and they didn't care two hoots who bought it so long as the check didn't bounce.

"And they got the car, too?" Leonard asked. "Even though you knew I wanted to buy it?"

"Everything in the house and garage," Sam said. "Lock, stock, and barrel. The whole nine yards. Everything but the kitchen sink."

"Actually, they got the sinks, too," Wilson Roberts said. "Kitchen, bathroom, and utility sinks."

"Yes, Wilson, I know," Sam said. "It's just a saying. *Everything but the kitchen sink*. It means they got everything."

"So is everyone in favor of selling the house?" Wilson asked. "Let's make it official."

Everyone mumbled, "Approved," except for Leonard Fink, who sat tight-lipped, frowning.

"Leonard, are you okay with selling it?" asked Wilson.

"I don't suppose I have a choice. You're going to do it no matter what I say."

"Can you offer a good reason for not selling the house?" Wilson asked.

Leonard couldn't, but didn't want to admit it, so fell back on the Bible, quoting an obscure passage from the Old Testament that had nothing to do with the matter at hand.

"So it's agreed, we'll sell it for two hundred and fifty thousand," Hank Withers said. "And the furnishings for an additional twenty-five thousand."

"One more thing," Sam said. "The superintendent is asking us to donate ten percent of the inheritance to the yearly meeting. What would you like me to tell him?"

"Tell him to stop being stupid," Hank Withers said.

"That Friend speaks my mind," said Wilson Roberts.

Sam phoned the superintendent after the trustees went their separate ways, and informed him a meeting had been held and the decision to sell the house made, and that a check from the meeting would not be forthcoming.

"What did the trustees say, exactly?"

Several days before, Barbara had reprimanded Sam for failing to speak the truth when it was difficult to do so. "Just tell the truth. You'll feel a whole lot better," she'd told him.

He thought perhaps this was a good time to honor her concern. "They told me to tell you not to be stupid," he said.

As it turned out, Barbara was right. Sam felt immeasurably better.

46

Sam took the next day off to help his mom and dad with their new home, spending the morning cleaning their yard, front and back, and the afternoon helping his mother organize her kitchen, placing seldom-used items in the upper cabinets she couldn't reach, his mother protesting the entire time that she didn't need his help, she could stand on a chair.

"And you'll fall and break a hip and I'll spend the next two months visiting you in the hospital and nursing home, so I'd rather take a few hours and help you now," he pointed out.

Sam's father spent the day in the garage, bemoaning the loss of his antique wrench collection, which was increasing in value as the days passed, and was now worth hundreds of thousands of dollars and worthy of placement in a national wrench museum.

Sam avoided the garage.

Jack Shear phoned that afternoon to ask if they could close on the house the next day. Sam called Ruby Hopper and Hank Withers to check their availability, then confirmed the time with Olive's lawyer.

"Are you free to disclose the buyers' names?" Sam asked.

"Not yet. You'll meet them at the closing tomorrow," Jack promised.

"They're legitimate, aren't they? I mean, they're not gangsters or something like that, are they?"

"No, no, they're a nice couple. Not married yet, but thinking about it. It turns out they knew someone in the meeting and thought it best not to reveal their identity until after the price had been agreed upon and the deal closed. They didn't want people in the meeting to think they had gotten a special deal just because they knew one of the members."

"That's kind of them, I suppose," Sam said. "No one can say we gave them a special deal."

The closing was set for ten o'clock in the morning, so after a few hours of work at the office, Sam drove to Jack Shear's office, where he met Ruby and Hank. They were a bit early, so took seats in the small lobby, chatting and reading magazines on wealth and investments, which depressed Sam, he having neither wealth nor investments.

Outside, a car pulled to the curb. Sam heard two car doors slam, then a moment later heard the muffled voices of a couple as they approached the office. The front door was pulled open, and Sam raised his head from a magazine to see his brother, Roger, and his girlfriend Christina Pringle enter the lobby.

Roger chuckled at the astonished look on Sam's face. "Bet you didn't expect to see me today," he said to Sam.

"What are you doing here?"

"What do you think we're doing here? We're buying Olive's house." He crossed the lobby and hugged Sam, slapping him on the back. "Isn't it great? Me, you, Mom and Dad, all within a few blocks of one another."

"Sam, is this your brother?" Ruby Hopper asked, stepping forward.

"Oh yes, let me introduce you all. I'd like you to meet my brother Roger and his girlfriend Christina Pringle. Roger and Christina, this is Hank Withers and Ruby Hopper. Hank is a trustee of the meeting and Ruby is our clerk."

"Pleasure to meet both of you," Christina said, reaching out to shake their hands.

"This is just wonderful," Ruby said. "It's so nice to see Olive's house going to someone we know."

"Are you related to the potato chip people?" Hank asked Christina.

"Not that I'm aware of," Christina said. "But I am a Quaker. Perhaps you've heard of my father, Otis?"

Sam wanted to hug Ruby Hopper for managing not to wince. "Oh yes," Ruby said. "I've known your father many years. I forgot he had a daughter. You're a doctor, am I right?"

"Yes, that's right. A pediatrician."

"How did you know about this house being for sale?" Sam asked. "We had barely listed it for sale."

"You mentioned it at Thanksgiving, remember?" said Roger. "So we drove past it on our way home and looked it over. The next-door neighbor gave us Jack Shear's name and number, so we phoned him and here we are. We didn't want you to know it was us. Me, I was all for telling you and seeing if we couldn't get a better deal, but Christina didn't want you to know it was us. Said it would put you in an awkward position."

"Christina, thank you for reining in my clod of a brother," Sam said.

Sam was elated. It had been close to thirty years since he'd lived anywhere near his brother. Now he was a five-minute walk away. Two minutes by car. Close enough to help their mother and father so Sam wasn't stuck with everything.

"Do Mom and Dad know?" Sam asked Roger.

"Are you kidding? Dad can't keep a secret. But don't you tell them. We want to."

"You go right ahead. But I want to be there. This is great. They're going to be tickled pink."

The closing went smoothly. Jack moved them quickly through the papers. Hank signed each one, along with Roger and Christina, then Ruby handed over the house keys and hugged the happy couple. "We'd be delighted if you joined us for meeting for worship on Sundays," she said. "It begins at ten thirty, then we stay afterwards for coffee and pie."

"Pie, you say?" asked Roger, clearly interested.

"Every Sunday," Hank Withers affirmed.

"We were planning to make Hope Friends our church home," Christina said. "We've let our spiritual life slide."

"What kind of pie?" Roger asked.

"Oh, whatever I'm in the mood to make," Ruby said. "This Sunday is strawberry rhubarb pie."

"We'll be there," Roger promised.

They celebrated the closing with lunch at Bruno's. Jack Shear's treat. An attorney springing for lunch, it was a day for miracles. Bruno fawned over Christina. "You Gardner men, you have such beautiful wives. If he treats you poorly, you can always leave him and marry me," he advised Christina.

"Actually, we're not married," Christina said.

"What's the matter with you, not marrying this beautiful creature?" Bruno said to Roger, cuffing him on the head. "A man should be married."

He returned to the kitchen, shaking his head and muttering under his breath.

"Don't take it personally," Sam told Roger. "The first time I met him, I thought he was going to poison me."

Bruno outdid himself, the food was incredible, and when he discovered Roger and Christina had just closed on their first house, he brought over a bottle of wine, filled everyone's glass, and proposed a toast to their happy future, but only after warning Roger that if Roger didn't propose to Christina within the month, he would.

47

~~

I'm glad we didn't know Roger and Christina were buying Olive's house," Sam said to Barbara that evening over supper. "I wouldn't want people to think they got a special deal. Especially since I was the one who called Ruby and urged her to accept their price."

"At least you know the truth," Barbara said. "But people are going to think whatever they want to think and someone is sure to bring it up. Probably the Finks."

"But Ruby and Hank were there. They know I didn't know."

"Oh, and you don't think the Finks aren't also suspicious of Ruby and Hank? Especially after that little dustup about the meetinghouse addition."

"Didn't think about that," Sam admitted. "Oh, well, in my own heart, I know I'm innocent of favoritism."

It was as if Barbara could peer into the future, for when Sam arrived at his office the next morning and downloaded his e-mail, a nasty little message from the Finks landed in his in-box, sent to him and every member of the meeting, accusing Sam of cutting his brother a deal on Olive's house. He ignored it. No use lowering himself to their level.

Hank Withers was not as restrained. He responded to the Finks, rising to Sam's defense, accusing them of speaking in ignorance, which was true but looked rather harsh when Hank typed it out in capital letters.

It got worse, not better, the rhetoric escalating until midday when Sam hit *Reply to All* and thanked the Finks for their concern, but said that he'd had no idea his brother and his girlfriend were purchasing the house, and suggested that e-mails were not the best way to discuss matters, that it was wiser to speak to people face-to-face, which he was happy to do if they wanted to come to his office, all the while praying they wouldn't.

Wanda phoned five minutes later.

"His girlfriend? They're not married? We sold the house to someone living in sin? I don't think the trustees would have approved the sale, had they known that."

"When a house goes on the market, you can't stipulate the morals of the buyer," Sam said. "Besides, my brother's relationship with his girlfriend is their business, not ours."

"The superintendent's going to hear about this," Wanda said.

All in all, it was shaping up to be a wonderful day.

"Call whomever you wish, but as long as we're speaking our minds, I don't appreciate your inference about my brother's morals. You've never even met him. But he and his girlfriend are coming to meeting this Sunday, so you'll get the chance."

"Let's just throw the doors open to sinners," Wanda said. "Is this your idea of church growth? Welcoming every bimbo and her lover?"

After dealing with Dale Hinshaw and Fern Hampton for

fourteen years, Sam was in no mood to put up with the same hateful nonsense at Hope Meeting.

"Wanda, if you're unhappy here, then I suggest you and Leonard find another church home. Because I'm not going to tolerate your unkindness to my friends and family. Do yourself a favor, do us a favor, and find somewhere you can be happy."

"I might just do that," she said.

"I think you should."

She hung up the phone. Sam sat at his desk, cooling down, thinking about Roger and Christina. It had surprised him to learn they were living together. He wondered if his parents knew yet. He wondered if Otis Pringle knew. Otis didn't seem like the type to let it slide without a sermon or two. And his mother would have pulled Christina aside to warn her about the man not buying the cow if the milk was free. Christina would probably have resented the comparison to a cow.

While Sam wasn't a prude, he was conventional about a few things and men and women living together without benefit of clergy was one of them. He hoped Roger and Christina married soon. Maybe he should talk with Roger. First he'd talk with Barbara. She was sensible about such matters. Maybe he could rope her into talking to Roger instead. That would be even better. Sam missed the old days, when people went out of town to sin and no one was the wiser, except for God, who was accustomed to such shenanigans and handled it better anyway. Every now and then smiting someone, but by and large forgiving them.

At supper that night, Sam told Barbara about advising the Finks to find a new church home.

"I hope they take your advice. They're miserable, and they're making everyone else miserable."

Then he asked what she thought about Roger and Christina living together. She was of the opinion that they were adults, that their relationship was no one's business but theirs, and that if anyone said anything to him, he should tell them that if they had a problem with Roger and Christina, they should speak with Roger and Christina.

"So does this mean you won't talk to them about getting married?" Sam asked.

"That's what it means," Barbara answered.

"At one time pastors' wives took care of such matters."

"At one time wives stayed home and families lived on one income. So if you want me to quit my job and we can live on your salary, I suppose I can."

"Let's not get carried away," Sam said. "I guess it's not our place to talk to them."

Sam couldn't remember the last time he'd won an argument with Barbara.

After supper Sam and Barbara went to visit his parents, curious what their response to Roger's situation might be.

"I'll tell you what I told Roger," his mother said. "I told him to go for it. Christina is a quite a catch and, quite frankly, I'm surprised she's dating him. You know your brother, he's rather immature. If he can land someone like Christina, more power to him."

"You don't think it's bad that they're living together without being married?" Sam asked.

"At one time it would have bothered me greatly," Gloria Gardner admitted. "Now I think it's arrogant of the church to say someone's love isn't genuine unless it's been blessed by the church. Doesn't that seem kind of Middle Ages to you, Sam?"

"Do you want to know my opinion?" Charlie Gardner asked, then plunged ahead without waiting for Sam's answer. "I say more power to him. She's smart, she's pretty, she's nice, and she's a doctor. He's set for life."

"Besides," Gloria Gardner said, "I think they'll be announcing a marriage before long, then it won't be an issue any longer."

There had been times when the only reason Sam had stayed a pastor was that he feared his parents' reaction should he quit to try something else. Now here they were endorsing free love and all sorts of wanton depravity. What, indeed, was the world coming to? Maybe Dale Hinshaw had been right after all. Maybe they were living in the last days.

"I'll tell you one thing. I'm a lot more concerned about you out walking the streets with Gretchen Weber, than I am about Roger and Christina," Sam's father said.

"Walking the streets with who?" Barbara said.

"Sam didn't tell you," Charlie Gardner said. "He's been exercising with Gretchen Weber. You know her. She's Ruby Hopper's niece."

"Was this before or after you had lunch with her at Bruno's?" Barbara asked.

"Can't we discuss this in privacy?" Sam asked.

"You had lunch with Gretchen Weber at Bruno's?" Charlie Gardner asked. "That was stupid."

Gloria Gardner frowned at Sam. "Are you cheating on Barbara?"

"No, of course not."

"I'm beginning to wonder," Barbara said. "He had lunch with her, and now you tell me he's going on walks with her."

"Just one walk was all."

"Before or after we talked about her?"

"Um, let me see, I can't remember."

Barbara turned to Sam's father. "When did you see them together?"

"Hmm, let me see, three, maybe four days ago."

And that, judging by the look on his wife's face, was the moment Sam Gardner realized he was a dead man walking.

48

Barbara held back until they reached home.

"Sam Gardner, I could wring your skinny little Quaker neck," she said.

"I know, I know. But she wouldn't take no for an answer. I only went once. You've got to believe me," he said.

"It would be easier to believe you if you had told me," Barbara said. "But no, I had to find out from your father. Do you realize how embarrassing that is? One more thing," she added. "I'm not mad that you went on a walk with another woman. You can be friends with women. I'm mad that despite our conversation about Gretchen, and my concerns, you didn't tell me. That feels dishonest to me."

He apologized profusely, acknowledging that he was the worst person on the face of the earth, deserving of a slow, torturous death, unfit for polite company.

"Oh, stop groveling," Barbara said. "Just stop acting like a moon-eyed puppy whenever Miss French Braid shows up. And knock off the walks. People are going to start talking. Geez, Sam, don't be an idiot."

234 · Philip Gulley

It could have been worse. He'd once read a story about an angry wife who'd sliced off a certain part of her husband's body while he slept. He didn't think Barbara would do that, but he slept with one eye open, just in case.

She was back to her usual cheerful self the next morning, but on the way out the door to do the grocery shopping gave Sam explicit instructions to stay away from Gretchen Weber if he knew what was good for him.

Sam showered, ate breakfast, then went to his office, where he found Ruby Hopper wanting to talk.

"Is it about Gretchen?" Sam asked.

"No, why would I want to talk about Gretchen? This is about the Finks. I understand you encouraged them to find another church."

"Yep, sure did," he said. "She said some hateful things about my brother and I kind of lost it. Told her she and Leonard would be happier somewhere else. How did you hear about it?"

Ruby sighed. "Wanda phoned me last night, very upset. They've been members here a long, long time. I hope it doesn't upset the others."

"You think anyone will be heartbroken if the Finks leave?"

"It's not that," Ruby said. "I just think some might be concerned our pastor took it upon himself to urge someone to leave. That probably should have been left to the elders to do."

"Not trying to be argumentative," Sam said. "But the elders have been putting up with the Finks and their hatefulness for decades now. Do you honestly think they would have ever challenged the Finks? They didn't say anything to Wanda when she had her outburst in meeting for worship last month. You had to talk with her. That's not even your responsibility, though I'm glad you did. Should have been done a long time ago."

"Maybe this is one of those times we should worry less about protocol and more about the end result," Ruby conceded. "You're right. They've not been happy for years and they're making everyone else miserable."

"It was actually kind of fun," Sam said. "I've never told anyone to leave a church. Have wanted to several times, but never worked up the nerve to do it."

"Well, let's not make it a habit. We're trying to get people in the meeting, not throw people out."

"Gotta break a few eggs to make an omelet," Sam said.

"Just so long as we remember people aren't eggs."

Sam smiled. "Point well taken, Friend. I don't want to be unkind to anyone. But I've made a habit of silence when others have been unkind. That is also a failing, don't you think?"

"Yes, I suppose it is," Ruby admitted.

Sam decided not to mention that Wanda had referred to Ruby and Barbara as "the idiots on the limb committee." No sense making matters worse.

"Hey, I have an idea," Sam said. "Why doesn't the meeting give me permission to give someone the heave-ho once a year? That way I won't get carried away with it."

Ruby chuckled. "Somehow I don't think they'll approve that."

"Well, then, I guess we'll just have to muddle through these things. Pull the bandage off slowly instead of ripping it off quickly and getting the pain over with."

"Have you ever known any church to do things the easy way?"

"You got me there," Sam said.

They chatted awhile longer, discussing their hopes for the meeting, and their private wishes concerning the inheritance, which was now safely settled in the meeting's bank account, earning a robust 2 percent a year.

"We'll need to spend some of it on a new roof," Sam said. "And the sooner the better."

"Wayne Newby is working on that even as we speak. He's interviewed three roofing companies so far. If he can just keep Hank Withers from installing a slate roof for a hundred thousand dollars, we'll be all set."

"Is Hank still gung ho on the meetinghouse addition?" Sam asked.

"I think he's settled down a bit. He is going to ask the meeting to set aside a portion of the inheritance for future meetinghouse expansion."

Sam thought for a moment. "That's not an altogether bad idea. Who knows, we might grow so much we'll need more room."

"We can always dream," Ruby said, smiling.

"Wouldn't that be fun?" said the minister who had never before been involved in a church building program.

49

Sam's sermon was finished, so he went home to Barbara. They went to a matinee, a movie Barbara picked, about a young mother who had been bitten by a poisonous snake and spent the entire movie dying in bed instead of getting her butt to the hospital for an antivenin shot. Sam was annoyed with the woman after the first fifteen minutes and was glad when she finally expired.

"Didn't you just love that part where she gathered all her family around her and told each of them what they meant to her?" Barbara asked on their way home. "That's the way I want to die. With all my family around me."

"If her family hadn't been such idiots and had taken her to the hospital, she'd still be alive," Sam said. "I hate movies like that."

"I suppose if I got bit by a snake, you wouldn't care how I felt about you, would you?"

"Frankly, no. I'd be too busy trying to save your life. Then when you lived, you could tell me how you felt about me. Don't you think in the two hours it took her to die, she had to be wondering why her family was too stupid to get help?"

"Sam, you don't know the first thing about love," Barbara said. "Men are always so practical."

"Call me crazy," he said. "But if someone gets bit by a poisonous snake, I'm not going to hold them and cry for two hours when I can make a phone call and save their lives."

"No one would make a movie about that," Barbara said. "People like drama."

Sam was starting to remember why he and Barbara seldom went to the movies.

"They didn't even kill the snake," Sam muttered. "Any snake I see, I'm going to lop off its head."

Sam hated snakes, and that night, instead of dreaming about Gretchen Weber, he dreamed of a snake falling out of a tree and landing on his head, only to waken and find Barbara's arm draped atop his noggin. It was four o'clock, but he couldn't go back to sleep, so he took a shower, checking the bathtub for snakes first, then got dressed and walked across to the meetinghouse to tweak his sermon, since a sermon was never really done. Sanded the rough edges on the closing story, threw in an extra Bible verse, added a joke, then stretched out on the office couch to grab some extra sleep, after looking under the cushions for snakes. Barbara woke him up three hours later, just as people were rolling in for Sunday school.

"No more snake movies for me," he said.

He was still thinking of snakes five minutes later when Wanda and Leonard Fink slithered down the front walk and into the meetinghouse.

"You're not getting rid of us that easy," Wanda said. "This is our church, too. If you don't like us, you can leave."

Starting the Sabbath by arguing with a fellow Christian at the entrance of the meetinghouse didn't seem appropriate, so Sam took the high road.

"Well, since we're both going to be here, then let's have a fresh start," Sam said, reaching out to shake Wanda's hand, which she took, but only after thinking it over.

"And Leonard, welcome to you also, Friend," Sam said, shaking Leonard Fink's damp, weasellike hand.

"Yes, yes, welcome, come in, Friends," Ruby Hopper said, swinging open the door to the meetingroom. "There's plenty enough room for everyone."

50

ou are such a wimp," Barbara said to Sam as they
walked home from meeting. "I would have given her the
heave-ho."

"Oh no, you wouldn't have. You would have done exactly
what I did. Put on a brave face, smiled, and made the best
of it."

"Not me. I'd have treated her like a snake and lopped off
her head," Barbara said, making a swift cutting motion with
her hand. "Ka-chop!"

"Then it's a good thing you're not a minister," Sam said.

Even with the Finks there, it had been a deeply satisfying
meeting for worship. Roger and Christina had been present,
along with Sam's mother and father. Otis Pringle had taken the
Sunday off from Harmony Meeting to help his daughter and
her boyfriend clean Olive's old house, their new home. He'd
come with them to worship.

"Christina has asked me to move in with them," Otis told
Sam afterward. "I'm not quite ready. Maybe in a year or so,
after my work is done at Harmony Meeting. Then I'll make

Hope Meeting my church home. Maybe give you a hand with ministry."

That was certainly something to look forward to.

Still, good things were starting to happen. Attendance had been picking up. The members of the meeting, or some of them anyway, had gotten in the habit of inviting their friends and family members to meeting for worship, and to their great surprise, some had agreed to visit, and a few had even re-turned.

Dan Woodrum had sat on the facing bench with Sam that morning, leading worship, and Libby Woodrum had read the Scripture verse, a passage from the Old Testament with un-pronounceable, complicated words, and pronounced all of them precisely, without hesitation. She had actually read the passage before worship, several times, practicing in front of a mirror, instead of reading it for the first time in the pulpit, stumbling from one word to the next.

"How did you like my sermon?" Sam asked Barbara.

"I could take it or leave it," Barbara said. "Didn't do much for me, but I've heard worse."

"Why do I even bother?"

"Oh, honey, I was just teasing. You know I like your ser-mons," Barbara said, taking hold of his arm. "If I didn't, I wouldn't listen to them every Sunday. You always give me something to think about."

"I'm sorry about the Gretchen thing."

"Let's not talk about that anymore," she said.

"Otis Pringle is going to move in with Roger and Christina next year and start coming to meeting," Sam said.

"Breathe deep, and concentrate on the good things that are happening," Barbara advised.

"Knowing Otis Pringle, he'll show up at my office every Monday morning to tell me how my Sunday sermon could have been better," Sam said.

"The first time he does, smile, take him by the hand, lead him from your office, and tell him you're not interested in having your sermons critiqued," Barbara said. "Easy-peasy. You just have to nip it in the bud the minute it starts."

"Back to our earlier subject," Sam said. "Were you surprised the Finks were there?"

"No, people like the Finks don't leave a church. They threaten to, but they just hang on and on, like a virus. But who knows, since you called their bluff this time, they might behave themselves for a while. I suppose if they get really hateful, you can try booting them out again."

They arrived home, changed their clothes, and walked the three blocks to Sam's parents' house for Sunday dinner. Roger, Christina, and Otis were already there. Christina was helping in the kitchen, while the men were seated in the living room, watching the Colts on Charlie and Gloria Gardner's new television set, their old one having been stolen. It was a huge television, the size of a small car, and Sam's father had the volume cranked up. Otis Pringle was still managing to talk over the announcer about his days as a high school football player.

"I thought about playing in college, they asked me to, but I wanted to concentrate on my studies."

"That's nice," Roger said.

"Yeah, I would have been a tackle. Did you play football, Charlie?"

"No, can't say I did."

"How about you, Sam?" Otis asked. "What's your sport?"

"I'm not much of a sports guy," Sam said. "I don't like to sweat."

The Colts were getting clobbered, so Sam excused himself and went to the kitchen and pulled Christina aside to show her a spot on his forehead he suspected was cancer, probably the start of a brain tumor.

"I don't think it's a tumor," she said, peering at it. "It looks like sun damage, though. I'd recommend you schedule an appointment with a dermatologist. We see a lot of basal cell carcinoma with men your age."

Carcinoma. Oh, my Lord, he was dying. This might be his last family dinner. At least it was fried chicken. He wished his sons were there. It would have been nice to see them one last time. He wondered who would conduct his funeral. Probably Otis Pringle. Barbara would feel obligated to use him since he was practically family. Otis would talk about himself, then rough people up a little, suggesting they weren't going to heaven, maybe implying Sam's eternal future was less than rosy, then coax a sinner down front, wrestle him to the floor, stick a knee in his back and make him give his wretched soul to the Lord. Christianity as a contact sport.

Sam decided to be brave and not let anyone know he was dying, at least during dinner. There was no sense dragging others down. They would find out soon enough. Apparently dying took a surprising amount of energy, because Sam was famished. He ate three pieces of chicken, two servings of mashed potatoes and gravy, green beans, orange Jell-O with carrot slivers, two yeast rolls, and a piece of blackberry pie, with a dollop of ice cream on the side.

"Ruby Hopper gave us the pie," Sam's mother pointed out. "She said it was our welcome-to-the-meeting pie."

"I wonder why we didn't get a pie?" Roger asked.

"Probably because you're living in sin," Sam said. He said it without thinking. It just came out. He supposed dying was causing him to be more direct.

"Sam, eat some more potatoes," Barbara said, spooning another mound onto his plate.

"Yes, about that," Otis Pringle said, turning toward Roger and Christina. "Any chance you kids will be getting married soon?"

It grew very quiet.

Very quiet, indeed.

51

Sam broke the silence. "It's probably none of my business, but now that I'm dying I don't have time to beat around the bush."

"You're dying?" his mother cried.

"I have cancer," Sam said.

"Said who?" Barbara asked.

"Christina."

"No, I said it appears you have a little sun damage on your forehead. It's not necessarily cancer, and if it is, it can be easily removed." Christina turned to Roger. "Is your brother always this paranoid?"

"Yeah, pretty much," Roger said. "When we were little, he spent a whole year thinking he had polio. It turned out to be eczema. But every Sunday for a month he stood during church and asked for prayer for his polio."

"I remember that," Charlie Gardner said. "He had the whole church thinking he was dying."

"But eczema is nothing like polio," Christina said, laughing. "Sam, what made you think you had polio?"

"If you're just going to laugh, I'd rather not say."

"He limped everywhere he went," Roger said. "He looked like Tiny Tim in *A Christmas Carol*. It was pathetic."

"We don't know that it wasn't polio," Sam said. "Maybe it was, and just maybe people praying for me caused it to go away."

"Was that the year you wanted an iron lung for Christmas?" Gloria Gardner asked.

"Yeah, he wanted an iron lung and leg braces," Roger said. "I remember that. You got him a bicycle instead, and he was mad at you."

It was obvious to Sam that Roger had raised this subject to deflect attention from his living in sin with Christina. Roger was slick, Sam had to hand it to him. But Sam was slicker.

"So how long have you and Christina been dating now?" he asked Roger. "Has it been four months?"

"Six months," Christina said.

"Roger, I proposed to your mother on our third date," Charlie Gardner said, smiling across the table at Gloria.

"Barbara and I were engaged four months after we met," Sam said.

Otis Pringle leaned back in his chair. "Christina's mother and I knew after our first date that we were going to marry one another. That was in October. By Christmas we were married."

"How old are you, Christina?" Sam asked.

"Thirty-nine."

"Not too late to have children," Otis Pringle observed. "Of course, you don't want to cut it too close. My mother had me when she was forty-one."

Roger was squirming. It served him right.

"Do you suppose we should get married?" Roger asked Christina.

"Oh, for the love of Mike, that's not how you ask a woman to marry you," Barbara said. "Put a little effort into it, a little romance. You might as well have asked if she wanted to have her teeth cleaned for all the emotion you showed."

"If I were going to marry you," Christina said, "I wouldn't want to be asked in front of your entire family, as if it were an afterthought."

"Geez, Roger, even I knew that," Sam said, though he was the one who had raised the subject of their possible marriage.

"What if the rest of us went on a walk and you and Roger were here by yourselves? Could he propose to you then?" Charlie Gardner asked Christina.

"Then you wouldn't be living in sin," Otis Pringle added, helping himself to another chicken leg.

"I'm not one to worry about what other people think," Sam said. "But it would sure save me a lot of trouble if you two were married. Otherwise Wanda Fink is going to be mentioning it every time she sees me."

"You've already bought a house together. Might as well tie the knot," Charlie Gardner said. "Besides, it'll help you on your taxes."

"Why do you assume Roger has to propose to Christina?" Gloria Gardner said. "This is the twenty-first century. Women propose to men, you know. Maybe Christina will propose to Roger."

"I don't think I'd marry a woman who proposed to me," Charlie Gardner said. "It doesn't seem right."

"Boy, if I had known that fifty-six years ago, I could have saved myself a lot of trouble," Gloria said.

"As it turns out, my next several Saturdays are free," Otis Pringle said. "I'd be happy to officiate, should you decide to get married in the next month or so."

"If Otis can't make it, I'd be happy to fill in," Sam volunteered.

There are few people who can withstand a frontal assault by two Quaker pastors, and Roger and Christina were beginning to wilt under the fire.

"It's not that we don't want to get married," Roger said. "In fact, we've even talked about it. We just wanted to spend more time together first. See how we got along seeing one another every day."

"I hope to be married one day," Christina said. "I would love to have a family. I just want to be sure."

"If you wait until you're sure about something, you'll never do anything," Otis Pringle said.

Gloria Gardner rose from the table and went upstairs. They could hear her rustling around in search of something. A few moments later, she called out, "Found it," then came back downstairs holding a small box.

"This was my mother's wedding ring set," she said, showing it to Christina. "When she was dying, she told me to give it to Roger. Sam and Barbara had already married by then."

"It's gorgeous," Christina said, admiring it. "Absolutely beautiful."

"Why don't you take it?" Gloria Gardner said.

"Hold on a minute here," Roger said. "Aren't I supposed to be the one asking?"

"Then get to it," Charlie Gardner said. "For crying out loud, I've never seen anyone dawdle the way you can."

Roger took the ring from his mother and turned to face

Christina. "So how about it, would you like to get married?"

"Oh, for Pete's sake, that's no way to ask a woman to marry you," Sam said. "Get down on your knee. Tell her you love her, that you can't live without her, and ask if she would give you the honor of being your wife."

"It's not like I do this every day," Roger said.

He dropped to one knee beside Christina's chair and took her by the hand. "I love you. I can't live without you. Would you give me the honor of being your wife?"

"Oh, brother," Sam said, "Not *your* wife, *my* wife. Say, 'Would you give me the honor of being *my* wife?'"

"Will you be my wife?" Roger asked Christina.

52

Everyone around the table watched Christina, who appeared to be deep in thought.

The silence was getting rather awkward.

"Maybe we should excuse ourselves, so Roger and Christina can have a little privacy," Gloria Gardner suggested.

"We're going to find out what she says soon enough anyway," Charlie Gardner said. "No point in leaving."

"This isn't quite how I imagined being proposed to," Christina said, finally.

"Caught you off guard, didn't I?" Roger said, smiling, as if proposing had been his idea all along.

"Are you sure about this?" Christina asked.

"Yes, I think you two are ready," Charlie Gardner said.

"Hush up! She wasn't talking to you," Gloria Gardner said. "She was talking to Roger. So, Roger, are you sure about it?"

"I'm sure," Roger said, turning toward Christina. "I'm sure I love you. I'm sure I want to marry you. I'm sure I want to spend the rest of my life with you."

Sam began tearing up.

"Then yes, I will marry you," Christina said.

Roger slid his grandmother's engagement ring on Christina's finger.

"Welcome to the family, Christina," Sam said, coming around the table to hug her.

"I guess this makes us family," Otis Pringle said to Sam. Sam wasn't sure how to feel about that, so just smiled.

"Now get busy and get us another grandchild," Charlie Gardner said. "Someone who can mow our yard and paint our house and take care of us in our old age."

Barbara began clapping, and everyone joined in. Roger blushed and Christina looked at her ring. "It really is quite lovely," she said to Gloria Gardner. "I'm honored to be wearing it."

"Roger and Christina, are you happy?" Sam asked.

"Never been happier," Roger said.

"Then now's a good time to tell you I put a dead person in the flowerbed in your backyard," Sam said.

"You did what?" Christina said.

"Put a dead person in your yard. Regina Charles. She wanted her ashes spread in her Aunt Olive's backyard."

"And when did you do this?" Roger asked.

"The day before you bought it," Sam said.

"We were going to put in a vegetable garden there," Christina said.

"I wouldn't do that for a while," Sam advised.

"I wish you hadn't scattered a dead person in our yard," Roger said. "How would you like it if I scattered a dead lady in your yard?"

"I would think ashes would be good for a garden," Charlie Gardner said. "Lots of minerals in dead people." He turned to Sam. "You can scatter dead people in my yard anytime you want."

"Thank you, Dad," Sam said. "I appreciate that."

"It would have been nice if you had asked Roger and Christina," Barbara said. "I wouldn't have wanted anyone doing that in my yard."

"I had no choice," Sam protested. "Regina wanted it."

"She's dead," Roger said. "What does she care? You could have flushed them down the toilet for all she knew."

Gloria Gardner pointed her finger at Sam. "No more scattering dead people on other people's lawns."

"I was just trying to help," he said.

"Help a woman who was suing us for a million dollars," Barbara said. "Sam Gardner, you never fail to amaze me."

"Jesus told us to love our enemies," Sam said.

"Love them, yes," Barbara said. "Scatter them in little pieces over someone else's yard, no."

"I read about this company in Texas that'll send your ashes into space," Charlie Gardner said. "Load 'em up on a rocket and blast 'em off. I'm thinking of doing that. I always wanted to go up on a rocket."

They discussed death for a while. Burial versus cremation. Sam was claustrophobic, so was leaning toward cremation and the comforting warmth of fire.

"How's the Lord going to resurrect you if there's no body to resurrect?" Otis Pringle asked. "I'll keep my body, thank you."

"This has been a thoroughly pleasant conversation," Christina said. "Not to mention romantic. A fitting dialogue for our engagement. I can't thank you all enough."

The men cleared the table and started on the dishes, as penance for being insensitive clods. The women retired to the living room to warn Christina of the challenges she faced being married to a Gardner male. If she had misgivings, she didn't mention them, which was kind of her, even though Barbara noticed she wasn't smiling as much. Roger was a nice enough guy, but Barbara wouldn't want to be married to him. Too passive. Too little ambition. And getting worse by the year. In ten years he'd be a slug with a beer gut, spending all his time in front of the television, talking back to the news anchors. He needed a good, swift kick in the butt and Barbara thought Christina was just the woman to give it. A high-heeled size eight right in the keister, pointed end first, lodged in the sphincter. It wouldn't be the first time a man had been set straight by a determined woman.

"What you have to do," Gloria Gardner advised Christina, "is take charge. If you wait for Roger to take the initiative, you'll wait a long time. He's my son and I love him, but you can't let up on him. If he sits down, he'll never get up."

Gloria Gardner had been praying for years that someone like Christina might come along and whip Roger into shape. She had tried as a mother, God knew she had tried, poured her heart and soul into it, but it hadn't taken. With Christina around, he was starting to step to. That's why she hadn't pushed them to marry. She was worried that once Roger snagged Christina, he'd ease up. But as she got to know Christina better, she began to think maybe Christina wouldn't stand for it. She had to hand it to Otis Pringle. The man had some juice in him. He was a few Pringles shy of a can, but he did have spunk, and it appeared Christina had inherited that virtue, and was smart to boot. A doctor! Her son was engaged to a doctor. Wait until the Quakers back in Harmony heard this.

53

In the kitchen, the men were talking, too.

"Otis, I don't mean anything personal about this," Charlie Gardner said. "Christina is a lovely young lady, but Roger, you're the man of the house. Take charge. If you don't, she'll have a ring through your nose in no time and she'll run you ragged."

"Man is the head of the household," Otis Pringle said. "I love Christina, but she's got her mother's personality. She's strong-willed. Don't get me wrong, her mother was a wonderful woman, but a little too independent. There were times I had to set her straight."

"Call me when you decide to set Christina straight," Sam told Roger. "I want to come see it. You got yourself a tiger by the tail. She's been single all these years. If you think she's going to roll over and let you be the head of the household, you'd better think again."

Charlie Gardner winced. "Your brother might be right. After a while, women get set in their ways."

"I wanted her to marry earlier, while she was still trainable,"

Otis Pringle said. "Your dad might be right. It might be too late."

"Are we living in the eighteen hundreds?" Sam asked. "Was there a time warp I was unaware of? You don't train a wife. It's not like having a dog."

"What do you think I should do?" Roger asked Sam, clearly anxious at the prospect of being married to a strong woman.

"I think you need to step up your game, Brother. Finish your college education. Get a job with a future. Shave off that patch of hair underneath your lip. Paint your house. Buy some new clothes. Learn how to talk about something other than sports."

"Maybe I should have waited before proposing," Roger said.

"If you had waited any longer, you'd be dead. Time to put on your big-boy pants and get married," Sam said. "Besides, being married is nice. Sure beats walking around the house talking to yourself and eating soup out of a can for every meal."

"The more I think about it," Otis Pringle said, "the more I think it's too late to train Christina. She's always been strong-willed."

"I could use someone with a strong will," Roger said, coming around to the idea. "Maybe it'll rub off on me."

"There you go, she's making you into a better person already," Sam said.

The men wrapped up the dishes, wiped down the countertops, and swept the kitchen floor, then went on a tour of Sam's parents' new house. Though Sam had already been through it a dozen times, he oohed and aahed in all the right places. But his mom had shoved some furniture around and hung curtains, and new carpet had been laid upstairs, so they noted that and went on and on about how nice the new house was, how it felt lived in and just like home already. It even smelled like his parents, like cream of mushroom soup, Sam thought, but didn't say.

His father took the men out to the garage to show them the workbench he'd built and where his antique wrench collection would have been if it hadn't been stolen.

"Did I tell you they caught the guys who did it?" Charlie Gardner asked.

"No, you didn't," Sam said. "When did you find this out?"

"A couple days ago," Charlie Gardner said. "I thought I told you. Are you sure I didn't tell you?"

"I think I would have remembered that," Sam said.

"Well, anyway, you know how I engraved my name on the wrenches? Turns out the bums sold them to a man who runs a flea market and Harvey Muldock came across them and called the police and the flea market man gave the police the name of the guy he bought them from and it was one of the thieves. He turned in the other two. One of their garages was full of stolen things, including our television set. But my wrench collection was gone. Sold off."

"Are you going to have give back your new TV set?" Roger asked.

"Nope, the insurance man told me to keep it," Charlie said.

"Look how the Lord took care of you," Otis Pringle said.

Sam thought maybe the Lord had more important things to do than make sure his father had a new television set, but he held his tongue. If Otis Pringle was going to be part of the family, Sam would have to let some things slide.

They trooped inside to discover Barbara on the phone with

Addison. They passed the cell phone from person to person, giving everyone the opportunity to chat with him. Roger told Addison he was getting married and asked him to be a pallbearer.

"It's not a pallbearer," Sam corrected him. "A pallbearer is for when you're dead. You want him to be one of your groomsmen."

"Yes, that's right. I knew that," Roger said. "Just a little nervous is all."

Addison agreed to be a groomsman, provided the Army would give him the time off, then asked to be put on the speakerphone, so he could tell everyone the news, which was that he had been promoted to specialist, which no one understood, but he seemed pleased, so they were happy for him.

"Is that the same as being a captain?" Gloria Gardner asked.

"Not quite," Addison said. "It's in between a private first class and a corporal."

"Well, I'm sure you'll be a captain before too long," she said.

They chatted with Addison a bit longer, then told him they loved him and couldn't wait to see him.

Barbara choked up talking to him. "Take care of yourself. Don't let anyone shoot you."

"Mom, no one's going to shoot me. I'm a medic on an army base in Texas, safe and sound. All I'm doing is checking people for herpes."

"Well, don't you get herpes. You behave yourself."

"I will, Mom. I promise."

Sam and Barbara said their good-byes and headed for home. The day had warmed, so they looped around the block, taking the long way home, walking their dinner off.

"This really is a nice place to live," Sam observed. "But I've been spending so much time at the church, I haven't had the chance to get to know the town."

"Maybe this summer when I'm off, we can get to know people," Barbara said.

"That would be nice," Sam said. "And I have to say, I didn't think I'd like having Mom and Dad right down the street, but I have to admit, it's kind of nice having family close. Now with Roger and Christina living here, it's even better. I really like Christina. I think she'll be good for Roger."

"I like her, too," Barbara said. "And I agree about your parents. I'd much rather have them living down the street than sleeping at our house."

"It was good hearing from Addison," Sam said. "I miss him."

"I do, too. We ought to drive out to Texas this spring and see him," Barbara said. "Maybe over spring break."

"Let's," Sam said.

They turned into the meetinghouse lane.

"Who's that in our driveway?" Barbara asked.

"I think that's Wayne Newby's truck," Sam said. "I wonder what he wants."

Wayne was seated on their front stoop.

"Doreen threw me out," he said. "She always said she was going to, but I never dreamed she would. Can I borrow your air mattress? I'll sleep in the living room. You won't even know I'm here."

"What happened, Wayne?" Sam asked.

"Oh, I kept one of the *Playboys*. Miss March, 1998. She has an overbite just like Doreen. Kind of reminded me of her when we first got married. Anyway, she found it and pitched me out. Told me not to come back."

Wayne's chin began to tremble.

"Why don't you spend the night with us," Barbara said. "We'll go talk with her tomorrow when she's cooled down."

Sam inflated the air mattress and made it up with sheets and blankets, fixed Wayne a sandwich, poured him a glass of milk, then turned on the TV to watch *60 Minutes*.

"I always liked *60 Minutes*," Wayne said. "Doreen and I used to watch it together." He began to weep.

Barbara patted his hand. "There now, don't cry. You'll be back home tomorrow night, watching television with Doreen."

"Maybe in time for *Jeopardy!*" Wayne said hopefully. "Do you think?"

"It wouldn't surprise me," Barbara said.

"I don't like Alex Trebek," Sam said. "He thinks he's God's gift to women. You can tell by watching him."

"Doreen thinks he's handsome," Wayne said.

"She can have him," Sam said.

"She also liked Merv Griffin," Wayne said.

"He wasn't any better than Alex Trebek," Sam said. "I wouldn't trust either one of them."

"Now Wilford Brimley, I really like him," Wayne said.

"Is he the oatmeal guy you see on TV?" Sam asked.

Wayne nodded. "Yep, that's the one."

"I like him, too," Sam agreed. "He seems like a regular guy."

With that issue settled, Sam and Barbara went to bed. It was early, but they were tired. It had been a long day. Good, but long.

They lay in bed talking softly so Wayne wouldn't hear them. "How long do you think he'll be here?" Barbara asked.

"Not long, I hope."

Barbara slipped her hand into Sam's. Sam thought how quickly life could change. Just a few days before, his marriage had been on the rocks, his life in jeopardy. Now he was for-given, his wife loved him, his sons were happy and healthy, Gretchen Weber was nowhere to be seen, Regina Charles was properly disposed of, and his brother was marrying up. Wayne Newby was asleep in their living room, but that probably wouldn't last.

Most all his life, Sam had been a worrier, had spent count-less hours fretting about one thing or another, only to be blessed time and again. Trouble he was ready for. It was good fortune that caught him off guard. *Maybe*, he thought, holding Barbara's hand and drifting off to sleep, *just maybe, there is a lesson in hope.*